"Maybe I Need A Sign Around My Neck Stating I'm An Adult," Angie Muttered. "My Brother Seems To Forget That."

"I don't think a sign will be necessary," Tyler told her as his eyes met hers. "You certainly look grown up to me."

Ty watched as a slight smile turned the corners of her mouth—the same delicious mouth he'd sampled the previous evening. He tried to clear his head of the thoughts, of desires that could only lead to trouble. His blood rushed hot and fast each time he came into physical contact with her. It was a sensation he wanted to pursue even though he knew it was forbidden territory. There was something about her.

Something he couldn't seem to put into words—something intangible that scared and excited him more than anything else ever had.

Dear Reader,

Silhouette Desire is starting the New Year off with a bang as we introduce our brand-new family-centric continuity, DYNASTIES: THE ASHTONS. Set in the lush wine-making country of Napa Valley, California, the Ashtons are a family divided by a less-than-fatherly patriarch. We think you'll be thoroughly entranced by all the drama and romance when the wonderful Eileen Wilks starts things off with *Entangled*. Look for a new book in the series each month…all year long.

The New Year also brings new things from the fabulous Dixie Browning as she launches DIVAS WHO DISH. You'll love her sassy heroine in *Her Passionate Plan B*. SONS OF THE DESERT, Alexandra Sellers's memorable series, is back this month with the dramatic conclusion, *The Fierce and Tender Sheikh*. RITA® Award-winning author Cindy Gerard will thrill you with the heart-stopping hero in *Between Midnight and Morning*. (My favorite time of the night. What about you?)

Rounding out the month are two clever stories about shocking romances: Shawna Delacorte's tale of a sexy hero who falls for his best friend's sister, *In Forbidden Territory*, and Shirley Rogers's story of a secretary who ends up winning her boss in a bachelor auction, *Business Affairs*.

Here's to a New Year's resolution we should all keep: indulging in more *desire!*

Happy reading,

Melissa Jeglinski

Melissa Jeglinski
Senior Editor, Silhouette Desire

Please address questions and book requests to:
Silhouette Reader Service
U.S.: 3010 Walden Ave., P.O. Box 1325, Buffalo, NY 14269
Canadian: P.O. Box 609, Fort Erie, Ont. L2A 5X3

IN FORBIDDEN TERRITORY

SHAWNA DELACORTE

Published by Silhouette Books
America's Publisher of Contemporary Romance

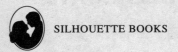 SILHOUETTE BOOKS

ISBN 0-373-76631-9

IN FORBIDDEN TERRITORY

Copyright © 2005 by SKDENNISON, INC.

This edition published by arrangement with Harlequin Books S.A.

® and TM are trademarks of Harlequin Books S.A., used under license. Trademarks indicated with ® are registered in the United States Patent and Trademark Office, the Canadian Trade Marks Office and in other countries.

Visit Silhouette Books at www.eHarlequin.com

Printed in U.S.A.

SHAWNA DELACORTE

Although award-winning author Shawna Delacorte has lived most of her life in Los Angeles and has a background working in television production, she is currently living in Wichita, Kansas. Among her writing accomplishments she is honored to include her placement on the *USA TODAY* bestseller list. In addition to writing full-time, she teaches a fiction writing class in the Division of Continuing Education at Wichita State University. Shawna enjoys hearing from her readers and can be reached at 6505 E. Central, Box #300, Wichita, KS 67206. You may also visit her at her author page at the Harlequin Web site—www.eHarlequin.com.

For Carol.
Your friends and family miss you.

One

Tyler Farrell's business partner barged into his office, panic covering his face as he pleaded, "You've got to help me out, Ty. Take her off my hands for the next few days."

"Take who off your hands?"

"It won't take that much of your time. She's just a kid."

"Who's just a kid?" Tyler's confusion began to turn to irritation. "What are you talking about, Mac?"

McConnor Coleman paused a moment as he took a calming breath. "All I know is what Mom said when she called the other day. It seems that my kid sister wants to move from Portland to Seattle, get a job and her own apartment. She arrived last night and is staying with me until I can help her get settled. I promised Mom I'd keep my eye on her. You know, maybe take her to a movie one evening and buy her some pizza.

Take her on the harbor tour or to the top of the Space Needle. Stuff like that.''

Mac renewed his determination. ''It's not like you'll have to put your busy social life on hold so you can wine and dine her. Like I said, she's just a kid. You know the kind of long hours I'm going to be putting in until this new design is finished. The pivotal point of our company's expansion plans is dependent on this design. I don't want her sitting all alone at my house and I certainly don't want her going out at night by herself.''

Ty made a valiant attempt to put some logic to Mac's obviously frazzled state of mind. ''We're on Bainbridge Island, not in Seattle. There's no reason why she can't go out alone.''

''A young girl should not be out on the streets alone.'' Mac's tone of voice said there was no room for discussion of the matter.

Ty allowed a slight frown to wrinkle across his brow. An image popped into his mind of Angelina Coleman, the annoying little girl he had encountered once at Mac's parents' house in Portland, Oregon. He shook his head and emitted a sigh. ''I really don't have the time—''

''Am I too early for lunch?''

Ty whirled around in the direction of the sound. The sultry voice perfectly matched the beautiful blond vision framed in the doorway. A quick surge of desire shoved aside Ty's initial shock. Could this gorgeous vision be the same person Mac had been referring to as his *kid sister?*

Mac rushed toward her. ''Angie…is it noon already?'' He glanced at his watch, a sheepish expression covering his features. "I guess the morning got away from me."

She shot a teasing grin at her brother. "Why am I not surprised?"

Recovering from his initial shock, Ty leaped into action. He grabbed Angie's hand, kissed the back of it and made a courtly bow. "Angelina Coleman...Tyler Farrell at your service. You probably don't remember, but we met several years ago." A jolt of charged energy emanated from their clasped hands. A heated surge of desire swept up his arm and through his body. Her unwavering gaze, combined with the vibrancy of her expressive green eyes, sent another ripple coursing through him—a strange combination of lustful desire and caution.

"I most certainly do remember you. It was fourteen years ago, a month or so before you and Mac graduated from the University of Washington. Mac was the one worrying about finals. I was the scrawny ten-year-old with braces on my teeth." A dazzling smile lit her beautiful face and a touch of humor surrounded her words. "And you were the arrogant jerk."

Ty released her hand, clutched at his chest and staggered back a couple of steps as if he had been hit by a mortal blow, his action eliciting a spontaneous laugh from her. It was an enchanting sound, one that left him wanting to hear it again and again. The moment he broke the physical contact with her a strange sense of loss made its way into his consciousness. Her words startled him, but they had been said more in fun than with any show of malice. At least that was the way he chose to take it.

He quickly recovered from the barb, taking a minute to make a survey of her physical assets. He judged her to be about five feet six inches tall, perfect for his six-foot frame. His gaze started at her mesmerizing eyes and visually traced every curve of her body until he reached the tips of her shoes. An appreciative grin tugged at the corners of his mouth. She certainly had everything and it was in all the right places.

A tightness pulled across his chest. His skin still tingled where their hands had met. He forced a casualness he didn't feel as he flashed a wickedly sexy grin. "Well...I'm happy to see that at least one of us has improved over the years."

Angie stuck her hands in the pockets of her tailored slacks, a subconscious effort to wipe away the sensation of his tantalizing touch. The devilish gleam in his hazel eyes told her exactly what was on his mind. It was a look she had seen on the faces of many men on numerous occasions, but it had never had this type of impact on her. It was a look that spoke of excitement and the promise of many nights of sensual pleasure for the woman lucky enough to share his bed.

It was a look that also spoke of fun, an open enjoyment of everyday things and life in general—something definitely lacking in her life for the past year. She wanted to regain that sense of fun that she had lost. She needed to have it back in her life.

Tyler Farrell was a very disconcerting man, yet there was something about him that she couldn't dismiss. It was more than his movie-star good looks, thick dark hair and strong athletic build. A little shiver of anticipation darted across the surface of her skin. She sensed an underlying level of passion that reached out and grabbed her like nothing ever had and refused to let go.

Angie glanced at her brother. An uncertain look surrounded by a hint of disapproval covered Mac's face as his gaze darted between his business partner and his sister.

Mac self-consciously cleared his throat. "Uh… Angie…about lunch today—"

Ty immediately took control of the conversation. "Don't give it another thought, Mac. I know how busy you are with the deadline on the design project. I would be honored to escort Angie to lunch in your place." He glanced at the delectable Angelina Coleman, then forced his attention away from the tantalizing image and back to his partner. He flashed a quick grin. "For the sake of the company and our expansion plans."

"I hate to interrupt your schedule, Ty. I can certainly amuse myself until Mac gets home tonight." His mention of expansion plans did not escape her notice. Hopefully the company's plans would fit nicely with her personal agenda, her primary goal—a plan she had not shared with her brother even though he was central to its success. It was her real reason for moving to Seattle.

Ty extended a dazzling smile and winked at her. "Nonsense. There's nothing I'd rather do than take a beautiful and charming lady to lunch." He glanced toward Mac before leaving, catching the look of warning aimed directly at him.

Ty escorted Angie out of the building. The tightness in his chest increased as the scent of her perfume tickled his senses. A sudden rush of discomfort left him uneasy. He felt pressured to make small talk even though he wasn't sure what to say to this enchanting woman who had just robbed him of his ability to be glib and charming. He took a deep breath. Maybe Mac thought of her as still being his kid sister, but there was no way this gorgeous vision could be thought of as anything other than all woman—beautiful and fascinating.

He took another breath and tried to brush away the flood of lascivious thoughts that invaded his mind. He tried to convince himself it was just force of habit. It was not as if he was entertaining serious thoughts about making a pass at Mac's little sister...not really. The band pulled even tighter across his chest. The heat settled low inside his body. Regardless of what he tried to tell himself, pizza and a movie were the last things on his mind.

The libidinous thoughts coursing through his head and pulling at his body were totally inappropriate under the circumstances, but that did not make them go away. She was Mac's sister, what Mac referred to as his *kid* sister—an expression that had a very protective sound to it, especially the way Mac said it. It was the type of sound that matched the look of warning Mac had shot in his direction.

Ty turned toward Angie. "Well...shall we go? There's a charming little place a short walk from here."

They strolled along the waterfront toward the harbor. As much as he tried not to, he couldn't keep from staring at her. He drank in her finely sculpted features, the turn of her nose, the absolutely delicious-looking mouth.

"Why are you watching me?"

Her words surprised him. His mind scrambled for some sort of acceptable explanation. "I...I was looking for similarities in appearance between you and Mac. I can see the family resemblance."

"I think we both look like our mother."

He allowed his gaze to drift across her features. ''You're not what I was expecting. I was still picturing that ten-year-old little girl.''

She emitted a sigh, part exasperation and part resignation. ''Yes, that's what Mac sees, too, whenever my name is brought up in conversation. He and Mom both. They're always patronizing me. I guess I can understand it. Not only am I the only girl, I'm also the youngest—the baby of the family with five older brothers. Mac is the oldest, thirteen years older than I am. I keep hoping that the day will come when they stop thinking of me as that little girl, but I don't think it's going to happen any time soon.''

Ty and Angie reached the restaurant. It was a bright, sunny autumn day and they were seated outside on the deck. After they ordered lunch he leaned back in his chair in an attempt to project a casual appearance, something far removed from the uneasiness churning inside him. ''So what have you been doing with yourself since you were that little girl?''

A teasing grin played at the corners of her mouth. ''Mostly I've been trying to get everyone to stop thinking of me as that little girl.''

Was she making fun of him? At that moment his mind was so muddled he didn't know what to think. His gaze slowly traveled across her features again, pausing a moment to take in the way the fabric of her blouse caressed the curve of her breasts. He finally settled on her tantalizing mouth, a mouth that deserved to be kissed long, hard and often.

''What else have you been up to besides not being ten anymore?'' His voice held a huskiness he wasn't happy with. He cocked his head as he made eye contact with her. A shiver of anxiety worked its way up his back followed by a shiver of uncertainty. Just pizza and a movie with Mac's kid sister—what had he gotten himself into? He was not sure about this anymore, not sure at all.

"I went to school. Then after I graduated from high school I entered an Oregon beauty pageant and was selected first runner-up."

He straightened to attention. "Ah...you're a beauty queen." He saw a momentary flash of irritation dart across her face.

"I didn't care about the beauty title. What I wanted was the college scholarship. I had some scholarship money, but it wasn't enough. I wanted to provide the rest of the funds myself. Unfortunately, with the heavy class load I had planned to carry I wouldn't have been able to work very many hours a week."

The words were not what Ty had expected to hear. She sounded very serious rather than simply engaging in casual chitchat. Was she always this serious? She had shown marvelous flashes of humor in the short time he had been around her. He was not accustomed to having serious conversations with women. "How did things turn out?"

"Mac came to the rescue as he always has for anyone in the family who needs anything."

The waitress interrupted their conversation when she placed the food on the table. Angie became reflective as she watched the waitress leave, then turned her attention back to Ty. "As Mac has probably told you, our father died when I was very young and Mac was still in high school. Mom had a tough time financially. She was raising six kids by herself and money was very tight. Mac worked for two years after he graduated from high school to earn the money he needed for college to supplement his scholarship funds. That's why he was two years older than the other freshmen such as you.'' She flashed a teasing grin at Ty and displayed another moment of her pointed humor. ''And far more mature than most of them.''

''Ouch!'' Ty expressed the pain of another direct hit to his ego, partly in good fun, but with an underlying layer of reality.

''Mac was right there for me. He stepped in and took care of the rest of my college expenses. I graduated with honors and a dual major in business and industrial design.''

Ty emitted a low whistle of appreciation. ''That's a very impressive accomplishment.''

''I never would have been able to do it without Mac's help. I've always looked up to him. He's been both my big brother and the father figure I never had. He always took care of me.'' She quickly blinked away the tears of emotion that started to moisten her eyes. ''I owe him so much.'' What she chose not to say was that she had always been in awe of Mac and his many accomplishments, not to mention just a little bit intimidated, too. She idolized her brother and knew there was no way she would be able to repay him.

She also knew he wouldn't accept it even if she could.

''Yes, Mac is a very generous and giving person.''

''Other than that, for the past three years since graduating from the University of Oregon I've worked in Portland at an industrial design firm. Unfortunately it was a job that didn't offer any challenges or any future.'' *Not to mention a boss who decided I was the office decoration and never took my work seriously.* It was a sore spot with Angie and an attitude she deeply resented. She wanted to be treated according to her merits, not her beauty. At one time she had even considered dyeing her hair in order to avoid being the object of the dumb blonde jokes. She quickly dismissed the idea. She was who she was and didn't see any reason to make changes just to appease someone else whose opinion wasn't important to her anyway.

Ty snapped to attention. Suddenly she was more than just a drop-dead-gorgeous beauty contestant. She was intelligent and articulate with a sense of humor and an openness that he found very refreshing, especially compared to a lot of the pretentious women he had dated over the years.

"Is your whole family close?" It was an area he had been both curious about and uncomfortable with—one in which he had no experience. "I know Mac feels very close to his family, even though he doesn't see any of them that often—which is not surprising, given his workaholic nature. He doesn't take near enough time for himself, time to just kick loose and have fun."

Fun...the word cut through to the core of Angie's reality. She stared at Ty for a moment. He seemed to her to be someone who knew how to have fun and enjoy himself—someone fun to be with.

"Yes. We're a pretty tight-knit family emotionally even if we aren't geographically close anymore. Only one of my brothers still lives in Portland. The others have moved to various places around the country in pursuit of their careers."

"What do you like to do for fun? What kind of activities do you enjoy?"

"Activities? Well, I like museums, concerts, art galleries and the theater. As for sports, I snow ski and water-ski. In fact, I enjoy just about anything connected with the water. I'm also the quintessential tourist. I love traveling and seeing new places.''

He nodded his agreement. ''I'd put sailing at the top of that list, which is fortunate since the design and construction of custom sailboats is the business we're in. Otherwise it sounds exactly like my choices.''

Angie took a couple of bites of her salad. ''We've certainly talked about me long enough.'' She shot him a quizzical look. ''How about you? What's your family like?''

Her memories of Tyler Farrell were from fourteen years ago. Even a ten-year-old could recognize an arrogant jerk with a roving eye for women. Judging by the way he had been looking her over for the past hour it was equally obvious that he still had that roving eye.

There was no question in her mind exactly what Ty was thinking. One glance at the devilish sparkle in his eyes and his wickedly tantalizing grin said it all. But there was more to Tyler Farrell than just the surface good looks. She sensed an honesty about him in direct contrast to the sexy gleam in his eyes and the playboy image he seemed to enjoy projecting. It was the type of honesty that said she would be safe from unwanted advances. He would probably make a pass, but he would accept no for an answer and not press her. And the same would be true even if she wasn't his business partner and best friend's sister.

Yes, when she was ten she had thought he was a jerk. A tingle of excitement heated her insides, telling her just how attractive she found him now. It had been six months since she had broken off her engagement to Caufield Woodrow III, a man her mother had kept telling her she should hang onto. A man who had everything—wealth, family position, social status and a guaranteed future. A man who could have given her everything she wanted. But Angie had disagreed. Maybe he could have given her everything material, but he had not given her any consideration for what she wanted out of life—it had been all about him and what he wanted…no one else.

And he didn't know how to have fun. She had never laughed when she was with Caufield. She liked to laugh. Everything had always been so serious with him. Everything had to be planned out well in advance. He had needed two weeks' notice to do something spontaneous. It had been a stifling relationship, one that had smothered her in a cloak of his creation. One in which she had finally realized she had been suffocated to the point where she could hardly breathe. She shook away the thoughts. It was old territory that she didn't want to go over again. She was relieved to be out of the relationship.

"My family…" Ty took a deep breath, held it a moment, then exhaled. The word *dysfunctional* immediately leaped to his mind. He was an only child who had been raised with money and privilege, but it was not a substitute for the type of closeness Mac had with his family—the type Angie had just described. The predominant memory from his early years was the constant fighting between his mother and father. His parents had finally divorced when he was in high school, but it hadn't stopped their ongoing battles.

And then there had been his disastrous two-year marriage shortly after he had graduated from college. Hardly a day had gone by without some sort of argument or at the very least enough tension to fill a football stadium. Family? A happy, loving marriage and close family was something he had never seen or experienced firsthand. It was something he would have said didn't exist if it weren't for the single exception of Mac and his family. But marriage and emotional closeness were things he would never know and he didn't want to try to capture it with another attempt at a relationship—an attempt he knew would be doomed to failure from the beginning.

He extended what he hoped would be a confident smile. "I was an only child, born and raised in Seattle. My parents both live in the Seattle area, my mother in Bellevue and my father on Mercer Island. I think that about covers it."

"That's certainly succinct and to the point." She returned his smile, letting him know she was not offended by his brief and evasive answer to her question even though she found it puzzling.

Lunch continued in a more comfortable vein. After the initial time of finding out a little about each other, the conversation turned to more casual topics and a surprisingly fun-filled two hours with lots of laughs. Each relaxed and enjoyed the beautiful day. Following lunch, they walked back to the offices.

"You know, Mac is going to be tied up for several days. My time is a lot more flexible than his right now so I'll be happy to show you around—" his gaze locked with hers for an intense moment, sending a heated wave of desire through his body "—if you don't mind the last-minute tour guide substitution."

"No…" A sizzling second of eye contact told her more than she wanted to know about the sexual magnetism of Tyler Farrell. A little shiver of trepidation tried to work its way to the forefront. "I don't mind at all."

"Do you have plans for this evening?" The tightness returned, like a band pulling across his chest, making it difficult for him to breathe. "I could pick you up at Mac's house at seven o'clock."

"That will be perfect."

Ty watched as she got in her car and drove away. He took a deep breath and held it for a moment. He slowly exhaled as he entered the building, crossed the lobby and walked down the hallway, but it did nothing to calm his inner turmoil. Angie Coleman had made a definite impact on his senses and he wasn't sure what to do about it.

He paused at Mac's office, leaning casually against the door frame. "I'm back from lunch."

Mac looked up from his work, glancing over Ty's shoulder. "Where's Angie?"

"She left. I suppose she went back to your house."

"Thanks for filling in for me and taking her to lunch."

"Don't worry about it, Mac." Ty flashed his patented smile. "It was certainly my pleasure."

"I'll have to make it up to her tonight. Maybe take her out to dinner or something." Mac glanced at the clock on his desk. "If I can get out of here at a decent hour."

"No need for you to quit earlier than you want to just so you can rush home to an empty house. I'm taking Angie out tonight." He cocked his head and tried to suppress his grin. "You know…pizza and a movie, just like you suggested."

Ty noted the cautionary look on Mac's face, but didn't want to start a conversation about it. He didn't want his business partner asking what his intentions were toward Angie. He didn't want to think about what his intentions were, to define the disjointed feelings and sensations that had been floating around inside him from the moment he had seen Angelina Coleman framed in the office door.

Angie checked the clock. She still had about an hour before Ty would be picking her up. She had spent the afternoon working on her resume. When Mac had told her he was busy and wouldn't be able to take her to lunch, she had been disappointed. She wanted the opportunity to spend some one-on-one time with him, dig into the operational procedures of the company, create a viable niche for herself in the organization, then pitch the idea to Mac about hiring her.

She wanted a job with Mac's company, but she didn't want him to hire her just because she was his sister—to once again come to her rescue, to take care of her. She wanted to prove herself to him and earn a job based solely on her own merit. She wanted him to respect her as a capable adult rather than protect her like a child. She wanted his approval.

Then her thoughts turned to Ty. If she had an ally within the company she just might have a better chance of Mac paying attention rather than in essence telling her to run along and play—to not worry her cute little head about anything. That was what had happened six months ago when she had first broached the subject of a job with Mac's company. She'd had her mother mention the job possibility to him. It was right after she had broken off her engagement. Her insecurities were at odds with her aspirations. She had been too scared and intimidated to approach Mac herself. All he had done was laugh and say how cute it was of little Angie to want to go to work for him. At that moment it was obvious to her that she needed to prove herself first if he was ever going to take her seriously.

Ty was not family. He wouldn't have any preconceived notions about who she was or what she should be doing with her life, what predetermined category she should fit in. She furrowed her brow into a slight frown for a moment. At least she hoped Mac hadn't put any preconceived ideas into Ty's head. If she could enlist his help, she was sure the two of them could get Mac to listen to reason and shed his old notions.

Angie glanced at the clock again, then put away her work materials so she could get ready for her date with Ty. She paused a moment, a reflective mood coming over her. Date...it wasn't a *date*. He was just being polite, seeing that she wasn't having dinner alone while Mac worked on his deadline project. That was all it was. Nothing more. She closed her eyes and an immediate image of his dazzling smile and good looks popped into her mind. The same sensation she experienced when he had clasped her hand began to spread across her skin. Her breathing quickened and a tingle of excitement told her there was something very special about this man whether she wanted it to be that way or not.

She brushed the last stroke through her hair just as the doorbell rang. She rushed to answer it, stepping aside as Ty entered the house.

"You didn't say where we were going." She glanced down at the simple skirt and blouse she had chosen, then made eye contact with him. The glint in his hazel eyes sent a little shiver through her body. "I hope I'm dressed okay."

"You look gorgeous." He forced a calm to his voice that he didn't feel as he blatantly stared at her. She was far more than merely gorgeous. She had brains and personality in addition to stunning looks. He had never been involved with a woman who had it all. Involved— that word had popped into his mind without him real- izing it. Where had it come from? He certainly wasn't *involved* with Angie. She was his best friend's sister, a best friend who also happened to be his business partner. A business partner who had managed to tell him "hands off" without ever saying a word.

He tried to shut out the feelings coursing through him, feelings that admittedly were mostly lust. But there was a hint of something else, too. Something he couldn't quite grasp or define. Something that made him nervous. His attention became riveted to her per- fect mouth, her slightly parted lips tinted with a soft russet color. He felt himself being drawn in against his conscious will.

He leaned his face into Angie's. It started as an in- nocent brushing of his lips against hers, but it ignited a burst of unbridled desire. Ty wrapped his arms around her and captured her mouth with a kiss that did nothing to hide the passion coursing through his veins. Her body stiffened in his arms followed by a moment's hesitation.

A touch of panic invaded his reality. Had he just made the most colossal blunder of his life? Was this going to cost him more than he had anticipated? Pos- sibly even the friendship of his best friend and business partner?

Two

Angie's initial shock quickly vanished. Ty's kiss held everything she had imagined it would and was everything she feared it might be. She slipped her arms around his neck and allowed the sensuality of his magnetism to flow through her. It was the last thing she had anticipated at that moment, but certainly not an unwelcome turn of events. Her thoughts faded into the background. Her breathing quickened. Her only conscious reality centered around his lips on hers and the fire he lit inside her. It was the type of heated desire her ex-fiancé had never been able to ignite in her, a sexy aura he had never possessed.

The kiss lasted for what seemed like forever before Ty finally broke the contact. It was a kiss unlike any she had ever experienced—a kiss that demanded more and promised everything in return. It was also a kiss that frightened her in its magnitude and the way it sent waves of longing crashing through her body. She took an unsteady step backward in an attempt to escape the lingering warmth of his embrace and the connection of their bodies pressed together. She nervously ran her fingers through her short hair. A kiss like that could only lead one place and she was not prepared to let that happen regardless of how attractive and desirable she found him.

There was a brief moment of eye contact. The intensity in his eyes sent a little shiver up her spine. It didn't matter how much she tried to convince herself that it was nothing more than an innocent kiss. She knew the truth was far removed from what she was trying to make herself believe. The ominous silence following their kiss grew louder and louder. She self-consciously shifted her weight from one foot to the other.

"Uh...where are we going tonight?" With any luck her words didn't sound as unsure to him as they did to her.

Angie's question broke into the thoughts running rampant through his mind—thoughts about the sensuality of this incredible woman and where the kiss was headed. He was thankful for the distraction. He started to speak, but a huskiness momentarily closed off his throat and no words came out. He tried again.

"I thought...uh, Mac had suggested...how does pizza and a movie sound to you?" He forced a smile that he hoped looked casual rather than something awkwardly pasted on his face.

"Pizza and a movie?" A teasing grin played at the corners of her mouth and an undeniable humor surrounded her words. "Yes, that sounds like Mac's idea of what his *kid sister* would enjoy."

She saw the quick look of hesitation dart across his face as if he wasn't sure how to take what she had said. She couldn't stop the laugh that quickly erupted. ''I happen to like pizza and I like movies. That sounds like a perfect evening's activity to me.''

And it was a perfect evening. Angie picked out a movie for them to see and afterward they went to a local pizza parlor. It was close to midnight when Ty pulled into Mac's driveway, then walked Angie to the door. He took her hand in his as he leaned against the wall next to the front door.

''Thank you for joining me tonight. I really enjoyed it.'' He suddenly felt like a teenager who was not sure how to go about ending a date. Should he try to kiss her again? Had it been a mistake to have kissed her the first time? Should he just leave? It had been a long time since he had been so unsure of himself. His dates usually ended in bed, but he knew that tonight would not be the usual. Tonight would be different, tonight he was with a very special lady.

''It was my pleasure. I enjoyed it, too. Would you like to come in for a few minutes?''

A quick rush of anticipation darted through his body. He stared at the closed front door for a moment, turning her question over in his mind. What was she expecting? Was he reading something into her invitation that wasn't there? Was Mac home? So far it had been a stress-free evening without the pressure of trying to impress anyone—just the comfortable situation of two people enjoying each other's company without the underlying layer of jockeying for control and pursuing ulterior motives.

He was very unhappy with the internal battle over which he seemed to have no control. He tried to gather his determination and regain the upper hand over his emotions. If her ability to kiss was any indication, Angie was definitely a woman who had not spent her life cloistered away from social situations or men.

She knew the score and had spent time out there in the real world of men and women despite what her brother preferred to believe. But that did not negate the fact that she was totally different from the women he usually dated. Maybe it was true that she knew the score, but there was no way she promiscuously slept around. She would be selective and when she did take that step it would be because it meant something special to her. A little shiver of anxiety told him she was definitely not the type he was accustomed to.

And then there was her brother. He had a responsibility to Mac that couldn't be ignored. The uncertainty ran rampant inside him, creating havoc and indecision, something that did not normally cross his life.

"Ty?" Her words interrupted his wayward thoughts as she repeated her invitation. "Would you like to come in and have a glass of wine?"

He searched her face and looked into her eyes. She was all fresh enthusiasm, trusting honesty and an underlying sensuality that had been driving him crazy from the moment he had encountered the adult version of the young girl he had met fourteen years ago. She was just the type who could sneak up on a man and have him fall head over heels in love with her before he knew it. Her type of woman was more dangerous than any predator—two-legged or four-legged.

As much as he wanted to ignore the realization and avoid the obvious, he knew she scared the socks off him. He also instinctively knew that he would never be able to walk away from her without returning. But as far as tonight was concerned...

The tremor of anxiety assaulted his senses again. "Well...uh, I think it would be best if I leave." It was the last thing he wanted to do. "I know Mac has been working long hours and I don't want to disturb his much-needed sleep." He may have been able to decline her invitation, but he could not stop himself from leaning his face into hers. But just as he was about to press his mouth to her lips, the front door swung open to reveal an irritated Mac dressed only in his pajama bottoms.

A startled Angie quickly stepped back, putting some distance between herself and the much-anticipated kiss Ty had started to initiate. She finally found her voice. "Mac...I'm sorry. We didn't mean to wake you."

Mac's gaze darted from Angie to Ty as he pointed to the wall where Ty had his arm and shoulder pressed against the wood siding. Mac's words held a caustic edge to them. "It was a little difficult to sleep with someone leaning on the doorbell."

Ty quickly straightened up, a guilty and embarrassed expression registering on his features. "I didn't realize it. Sorry about that." He glanced at Angie, gave her an apologetic smile and turned back to Mac. "I was just leaving. I'll see you in the morning."

Ty waited until Mac went back inside the house, then again turned his attention to Angie. His voice became soft, matching his warm smile. "Thank you for spending the evening with me. I thoroughly enjoyed it. I'll call you tomorrow."

Angie watched as Ty returned to his car, backed out of the driveway and drove down the street. She went inside the house and closed the door.

She turned a questioning look toward her brother who had not gone back to his bedroom. She noted his nervousness and awkward mannerisms. ''What is it, Mac? What's bothering you?''

''I'm not trying to pry into your life—''

''Uh-oh…here comes the *but*.'' Angie cocked her head and leveled a steady gaze at him. She made an unsuccessful attempt to suppress the teasing grin that flirted with the corners of her mouth. ''But, what? What is it you want to say that really isn't prying into my personal life?''

He ran his fingers through his sandy-brown hair, then shifted his weight from one foot to the other. ''It's…uh…it's nothing really. I just, well, I just wanted to say a couple of words about Ty.'' He cleared his throat, a nervous mannerism she had associated with her brother for as long as she could remember.

Mac tried again to say what was on his mind. ''Ty has a certain reputation where women are concerned.'' He glanced away for a moment, as if trying to gather his thoughts. ''It's not that he's really a womanizer in the true sense of the word. He isn't a love-'em-and-leave-'em type, but he does seem to always be dating someone new and never settles down. He's the type of man who has had lots of experience with lots of women.'' He managed to hold eye contact with her in spite of his obvious embarrassment over the subject. ''He's the type of man you haven't had any experience with.''

He gave her a brotherly hug. ''I just want you to be on your toes and not be taken in by his charm and smooth lines.''

''Are you trying to say that Ty would make improper

advances toward me and refuse to take no for an answer?''

''No, that's not what I'm saying,'' he said, a frown of concern wrinkling his forehead, ''not exactly. It's just that Ty travels in the fast lane. What is commonplace for him is way out of your realm of experience. I'm worried about you being able to handle what might be an…uh…well, an awkward situation.''

She could see her brother's discomfort in trying to deal with the topic in a dispassionate way. She also saw his deep and sincere concern. Her spontaneous laugh filled the living room. ''Do I need to remind you that I grew up with five brothers and learned how to take care of myself around a bunch of unruly guys?''

''Okay.'' He returned her smile. ''Enough said.'' He gave her a kiss on the forehead and returned to his bedroom.

Angie hurried down the hall toward the guest room where she was staying. She didn't know whether to be amused or annoyed by Mac's attempt to protect her. She had almost asked him if he really thought she was still a virgin, but decided against it. She didn't want to totally shock his sensibilities where his kid sister was concerned. However, his words about Ty's antics with lots of women did not escape her attention.

Thoughts of Ty flooded her mind, sensual thoughts that seemed to come from nowhere and insisted on lingering in her consciousness. She felt confident she could get him to help her convince Mac that he needed to hire her, but using her feminine wiles to manipulate a man was not part of her nature and certainly not the way she wanted to approach this problem. A quick stab of guilt poked at her, touching on her deeply buried insecurities. She was not a deceptive person, nor was she dishonest.

So why was this guilty feeling jabbing at her? She was not using Ty. She would never do that type of unethical thing, but if he could help her, why shouldn't she explore that possibility? She tried to shake away the guilt as she touched her fingertips to her lips, reviving all the heat and passion of the original kiss. A moment later any thought of a job with Mac's company, trying to get her priorities straight or her true interest in Ty and whether she was trying to use him totally left her head. Logic…thoughts…concerns… none of it mattered. Her entire reality at that precise moment was filled with the remembered sensation of Tyler Farrell's lips against hers and the heated desire he stirred in her.

Angie undressed and went to bed, but sleep did not come easily. Her thoughts continued to center around Ty and the heated moment they had shared earlier that evening. She knew she could not allow this sexy man to sidetrack her from her goals.

She had allowed her ex-fiancé to make decisions for her. It had resulted in a disastrous relationship. She had vowed to never again put herself in that position. It was up to her to set her life on a forward moving track and secure her future. That was her goal. She gathered her determination. It was her only goal. She would not be dissuaded from it—certainly not by a handsome playboy whose kiss made her skin tingle, her pulse race and her heart pound.

She turned over, pounded her pillow into a comfortable shape and closed her eyes. She finally succumbed to a restless sleep filled with images of the very sexy and desirable Tyler Farrell.

* * *

The next morning Angie wandered into the kitchen to make some coffee after taking her shower. She paused when she saw the note stuck to the refrigerator door. She looked at the clock. There was no getting around her brother's workaholic nature. Not even seven o'clock yet and he was already gone. She shook her head and furrowed her brow as she read the note.

> Angie: Lots to do. Will be buried under a ton of work the next few days. Hope you didn't mind too much being stuck with Ty yesterday. As soon as I finish this design project I'll be able to spend time with you, help you get settled into your own apartment and find a job. I think one of our clients has an opening in his company for a receptionist. Come by the office and I'll try to make some time to have lunch with you.

Angie scanned the note again with a soft sigh of resignation. Nothing had changed. A receptionist job—it was obvious Mac didn't have a clue what type of job she wanted, what she was qualified to do and what type of work experience she had. His only thought was to help her find an entry-level office position somewhere. How typical of Mac. He assumed she only wanted a job until she could find a husband rather than wanting to build a career for herself.

Then she turned her attention to the other part of the note. A little grin tugged at the corners of her mouth. Did she mind being stuck with Ty? He might as well have asked her if she minded if Prince Charming paid a little bit of attention to her. A shiver of trepidation accompanied her thought and was followed by a sudden rush of excitement at the memory of the passionate kiss they had shared. She tried without success to dismiss the heated desire the memory evoked. Maybe it would be better if she found some other way of achieving her goal rather than spending a lot of time with Tyler Farrell in an attempt to elicit his help.

And maybe tomorrow Prince Charming would sweep her off her feet and declare his undying love for her.

Angie felt her eyes widen in shock at the full impact of the errant thought that had invaded her consciousness. She didn't know where it came from, but she certainly needed to get rid of it as quickly as possible. She renewed her determination. One kiss did not mean anything. It was an enjoyable little interlude and that was it. She would let Ty know her areas of expertise and show him she was qualified for a responsible position with the company. In a few days Mac would be finished with his project and she could talk to him about it, too. Plain and simple. She breathed a sigh of relief. What felt out of control a few moments ago was now reined in and controlled.

Angie busied herself around the house until midmorning, then dressed and went to Mac's office. No sooner had she entered the lobby than someone grabbed her arm and spun her around. She found herself looking into the handsome features and bright hazel eyes of Tyler Farrell. His devilish grin sent little tremors through her body. The place where his hand rested on her arm radiated a sensual warmth.

"This is quite a coincidence. My lunch meeting just cancelled out on me so I have the next few hours free. I was just about to call to see if I could persuade you to have lunch with me. I already have a reservation at the Space Needle. Perhaps we could do the harbor cruise after lunch.'' Ty cocked his head and raised an eyebrow. "So…are you available?''

He flashed a devastatingly sexy smile and she melted on the spot. "Lunch?'' She suddenly felt like a fifteen-year-old, all tongue-tied and flustered in the presence of the captain of the high school football team. She pulled in her rampaging desires and did her best to project a calm, confident persona. "Yes, I'd love it.'' She tried to convince herself there was nothing wrong in having lunch with him again. It was nothing personal. After all, she had to eat anyway and Mac had asked Ty to take her sightseeing while he was busy.

She would keep the conversation turned to business in general and specifically to available or upcoming positions in the company. Ty's comment the day before about the company's expansion plans hinging on Mac's design continued to swirl around in her mind. Expansion meant new jobs, possibly in areas that did not currently exist. It was a perfect time for her to put in her bid for one of those newly created positions.

But in the meantime there wasn't anything wrong with an innocent afternoon of fun.

Ty's voice cut into her thoughts. "We have a little while before lunch. Has Mac shown you around our facility?''

"No, I haven't seen anything beyond the lobby and offices.''

"Would you like a tour? I could show you around the design room, the lab and the shop where we do the actual boat construction.''

Her entire manner leaped to rapt attention. "I'd love to have a guided tour.'' It was perfect. She would have an opportunity to see how things worked, get more of a technical tour than Mac would ever take the time to give her. She could ask Ty questions she couldn't ask Mac and certainly get more useful answers than her brother would give her. It would be the perfect setting to start her campaign to win Ty over to her side. She was certain Mac would listen to Ty. After all, Ty was his business partner in addition to being his best friend.

Ty escorted her through the lobby and down a hallway, pausing a minute at the door to Mac's office. "I'm going to take Angie on a tour of the facility."

Mac looked up from his work, then glanced at his watch. "Yes, a tour would be nice." He looked at Angie. "I'm sorry I haven't had any time to spend with you."

"I assume this means lunch is out?"

A sheepish expression crossed his face. "I'll try to be home for dinner."

"No need to worry about Angie being alone for dinner. I'll take her out to grab something to eat."

She glanced questioningly at Ty for a moment. He hadn't mentioned anything about dinner. She returned her attention to her brother. "He's right. There's no reason for you to pull yourself away from your design project before you're ready. You stay and work as late as you need to and don't worry about me." She glanced at Ty. "I'll be in good hands."

An involuntary glance toward Mac told Ty what he didn't want to know. Mac's expression was neither gracious nor distracted. Unlike many occasions when Mac's thoughts had him so preoccupied he didn't notice what was going on around him, this time there was no mistaking the fact that he was fully aware of his surroundings. It was obvious to Ty that Angie's comment about being in good hands had caught Mac's undivided attention.

Ty turned toward Angie. "Are you ready for the VIP tour?"

"Ready and willing." A little shiver of something, she wasn't sure what, told her she might be ready and willing for a lot more than a tour of the building and a business lunch.

They left Mac's office and Ty spent an hour showing her what they did and how they did it. Each step started with Mac's initial design, computer testing of the design, a miniature model, tank testing of the miniature, then the finished product custom-built for the client. She was very pleased with the way Ty assumed she'd understand what he was talking about and didn't reduce everything to the level of a ten-year-old.

The phase of the process she found most interesting was the design of the interior areas such as cabins and galleys so that they made maximum functional use of the space available yet were still attractive. They had a computer program that allowed the customer to see what the interior would look like with different fabrics, colors, woods and fixtures rather than simply picking something from a catalogue without being able to see it as part of the whole.

After the tour Ty and Angie took the ferry across to Seattle. They enjoyed a leisurely lunch in the revolving restaurant at the top of the Space Needle. The bright sunny day provided views of the Olympic mountains to the west and the Cascades to the east with Mt. Rainier looming large on the horizon to the southeast. The mountain views served as a spectacular backdrop to the water and greenery of Puget Sound and the expanse of the Seattle metropolitan area.

Conversation was casual, but far more superficial than she wanted it to be. She made several attempts during lunch to turn it to business matters while pursuing her goal. And each time he managed to deftly switch to a different topic.

Angie toyed with the stem of her wineglass as she made another attempt to procure information about the company. "Did I hear you correctly yesterday when you said something to Mac about the outcome of his design project having an impact on expansion plans for the business?"

Ty took a sip from his wineglass before answering her, as if he was determining how much to say. Or perhaps it was her guilty conscience that made it seem that way.

"The company is at a crossroads at the moment. Either we undertake a costly expansion which will include physically moving the location of the business to much larger facilities in order to meet our potential, or we scale back so that we continue to maintain what we have. It's the results of Mac's design project that will pretty much make that decision for us. If the design he's working on is successful, then we can move into the arena of the design and construction of larger sailboats in the luxury yacht category. We already have some of the ancillary support systems in place such as the computerized interior design enhancement I showed you this morning."

This bit of information leaped out at Angie. Everything about the interior design system had fascinated her. Perhaps that was the area where she should concentrate her efforts, something that would fit nicely with her education and work experience in industrial design. Her excitement over this new facet filled her with questions.

"Would this interior design work be done primarily outside the company or is it something you plan to keep in-house as a department of the newly expanded operation?"

"It's too soon to say. We're taking it one step at a time, and right now the step we're handling is the completion of the design Mac is working on. I've already done my preliminary work. I've talked to clients and business associates and have determined that the potential business is available. Our bankers have assured me they're interested in providing the needed capital for the expansion. But until Mac finishes the design and we successfully test it, everything else is only speculation."

"What clients do you have who would be interested in purchasing a custom-designed luxury sailboat? You said you'd need to move the facility to another location. Would you still remain in the Seattle area? Do you think—" She saw the look of caution dart across his features. Had she gone too far? Was she pushing too much? The look of caution slowly turned to a stern gaze, tempered slightly by the wry twinkle in his eyes.

"If I didn't know better I would swear you were an industrial spy trying to pump me for information about our development projects and the names of our clients."

She felt the heat of embarrassment sear across her cheeks. His accusation shocked her. Well, it wasn't really an accusation as such, but more of a half serious, half teasing observation. But it was serious enough that it made her realize she had pushed him too hard in her zeal to gather information.

"I'm sorry, I didn't mean to sound like that. It's just that I'm interested and Mac always talks in such general terms. He probably thinks I wouldn't understand what he was talking about even though I keep reminding him that I have a degree in business and industrial design plus three years of practical work experience at an industrial design firm." She offered a confident smile, hoping it would help sidetrack Ty's sudden concerns. "Maybe I should wear a sign around my neck stating that I'm an adult and don't need to be patronized."

Ty's response was a measured but easy laugh. "I don't think a sign will be necessary." His smile slowly faded as their gazes locked in a heated moment of desire. "You certainly look all grown up to me."

She silently berated herself for being too aggressive in her questions. She would need to be more subtle in enlisting Ty's help. If only Mac hadn't laughed at her six months ago when she had first worked up the courage to express her desire to work for his company. It would have made things so much easier for her now.

Ty would be a good conduit for swaying Mac's initial reaction to her working for the company, but that wouldn't make Mac realize she was no longer a child to be patronized and protected. It was a dilemma she knew she would be wrestling with again and again just as she was now wrestling with her intense attraction to Tyler Farrell.

After lunch they walked along the waterfront area. Each time he touched her—placing his hand at the small of her back to help guide her through a crowd, innocently draping his arm around her shoulder as they walked along the sidewalk, tugging on her hand to stop her when he wanted to point out a specific sight—a tremor of excitement rippled through her body followed by a warm sensuality that settled inside her.

But oddly enough, the excitement was tempered with a feeling of closeness. It was a special combination she had never experienced with anyone else, but one she found appealing and very comfortable. A hint of concern tried to work its way into the warmth surrounding her, a warmth that suddenly felt far too comfortable. She couldn't afford to lose sight of her goal.

"How about a harbor cruise?" Ty's question broke into her thoughts, jerking her back to the moment at hand.

"Sounds like fun." Her words said one thing, but reality was something else. She knew spending more time with Ty could only lead to complications in her life, complications she didn't want or need at this time.

A few minutes later they boarded the boat for the tour of Elliott Bay. The ocean breeze ruffled through her hair. The crisp air tickled her senses. She closed her eyes and drew in a deep breath, held it for several seconds, then slowly exhaled. "I love being on the water. It always makes me feel so relaxed." A cloak of calm and serenity settled over her.

Ty watched as a slight smile turned the corners of her mouth—the same delicious mouth he had sampled the previous evening. The same mouth that tasted of more and held the promise of tantalizing pleasures yet to be. He tried to clear his head of the ill-advised thoughts, of desires that could only lead to trouble. She was his best friend's sister…his business partner's sister…someone who should logically be off-limits. Yet he felt drawn to her on every level as he had never been with anyone before.

She definitely pushed every lustful button he possessed. His blood rushed hot and fast each time he came into physical contact with her. It was a sensation he wanted to pursue even though he knew it was forbidden territory. But there was more than merely wanting to get her into his bed for a night of unbridled passion—for *many* nights of unbridled passion. There was something else about her. Something that would not crystallize into a clear thought. Something he couldn't seem to put into words—something intangible that scared him more than anything else ever had.

Three

The next night Angie and Ty strolled hand in hand up the walkway to Mac's front door. Her enthusiasm showed in her voice. "Thank you for the play. I love theater and really enjoyed this production."

"It was my pleasure. I'm glad you were able to go with me."

The house was dark, but they could see Mac's car through the garage window. Ty gave her hand a little squeeze. "Mac's probably asleep. He's been putting in long hours for the past several days." He indicated the two chairs on the porch. "Let's sit here rather than going inside. Our conversation out here won't wake him."

Angie sat down. Ty scooted the other chair next to hers before sitting. She pursed her lips as if concentrating on something, then cocked her head and stared at Ty for a moment with her brow furrowed in thought.

"I think he works too hard. Perhaps what he needs is some sort of personal assistant…an administrative assistant. Someone different than a secretary, with completely different duties. Someone with the expertise to comprehend his design projects and know how design works, someone who has the knowledge to understand conceptually how what he does relates to the business end.''

She knew she was grasping for straws, trying to pull the proverbial rabbit from the hat. She wanted to establish as many possible career opportunities for herself as she could. Surely one of them would capture Mac's attention and be something she could build on in her pursuit of a solid career move.

Ty squirmed uncomfortably in his chair. Once again she had turned their conversation to the company as she had done on several occasions over the past three days and he wasn't sure why. He didn't know exactly how to respond. "Well, that's an interesting description of a job.''

She flashed a sparkling smile, one she hoped appeared more casual than it felt. "Perhaps that's something to keep in mind when you get down to serious discussion of your expansion plans.''

A soft chuckle escaped his throat, one that belied the caution in his eyes. "If I didn't know better I'd swear you were putting in your bid for a job with the company. But, of course, that would be ridiculous. If you want a job all you need to do is tell Mac and I'm sure he'd hire you.''

"Well…now that you brought it up…''

Her words faded from his mind. A tightness pulled across his chest as the heat rose in his body. The streetlight provided just enough illumination to highlight her delicately sculpted features. He put a stop to any further discussion of company business, or anything else for that matter. He pulled her into his arms and captured her mouth with a kiss that quickly exploded with the passion that seemed to always be simmering just below the surface whenever he was close to her.

Her taste was as addictive as any narcotic. No matter how many times he kissed her, he knew it would never be enough. He ran his fingers through the silky strands of her hair, caressed her shoulders, then pulled her from the chair and onto his lap. A warning tried to push through his sensually fogged mind, but he shoved it away. At that moment he didn't want anything to interfere with his pursuit of the captivating Angelina Coleman.

His breathing quickened. He knew exactly where he wanted this to go. He tightened his embrace, pulling her body closer to his. He felt her breasts press against his chest with each breath she took. He brushed his tongue against hers, reveling in the texture and the intimacy of the action. The kiss deepened as the level of sensuality surged through his body. The tingle of excitement rippled across his skin when she brushed her fingers against the back of his neck, then ran them through his hair.

More than anything he wanted to whisk her away to his house and spend the night making passionate love. But as much as that was what he wanted, he knew it couldn't be. It was a topic he did not want to delve into any further, an internal battle he feared would be his undoing. He had any number of women who had been in his bed and would willingly be there again. All he needed to do was pick up the phone and dial. But that wasn't what he wanted. Not one of them could measure up to Angie.

He reluctantly broke the kiss, but couldn't stop himself from lingering a moment longer with his lips brushing softly against hers. He knew he had to leave before it was too late and he did something he would end up regretting.

He fought for control over the desire and emotion he feared would show up in his voice. "Angie..." He brushed another kiss against her lips, allowing his hand to slip from her back and come to rest on her hip. He suppressed a sigh of resignation, not wanting to show how much he didn't want to say what he knew had to be said. "It's getting late. I have an early-morning breakfast meeting in Seattle with the client who cancelled yesterday's lunch meeting. I think I'd better head for home so I can get some sleep. I need to be bright and alert first thing in the morning."

He had never felt so out of control with what he wanted and so attracted to what he knew he couldn't have. An image of Mac's warning look popped into his mind, unwanted and unwelcome. He felt as if he was walking a tightrope stretched between his desires on one side and his loyalties on the other side, without a safety net to catch him if he made a misstep. No matter which direction he went, he would end up losing something special and important. And like it or not, he had to admit that Angie was someone very special and with each passing hour was becoming more important to him.

Angie stood up and took a step back to distance herself from the magnetic pull of Tyler Farrell. Her hand involuntarily went to her kiss-swollen lips, the heat of his passion still searing her. She had never been kissed the way Ty kissed her, had never experienced that type of toe-curling excitement. If they gave prizes for kissing he would possess every trophy available. Her thoughts strayed to what it would be like to have Ty make love to her. It was not the first time that notion had popped into her mind and she knew it wouldn't be the last. She also knew it was not a very wise idea regardless of how exciting a prospect it would be.

He grasped her hand as he stood up, sending a sensual flow rushing through her body. She stepped closer to him, resting her other hand against his chest. "Yes, it's getting late." She didn't like the breathless quality of her voice. It betrayed far more than she wanted to show. "That early-morning breakfast meeting will be here before you know it."

"We're scheduled to meet at seven o'clock." He glanced at his watch with a self-conscious smile. "And that's a little earlier than I like."

She took a step toward the door, allowing her hand to remain in his grasp a little longer. She didn't want him to leave. She didn't want to lose the warmth of his touch. "I know what you mean. Seven o'clock isn't that early but to be up and ready, catch the ferry for that thirty-five-minute ride to Seattle, then drive to the restaurant in time for your meeting is another matter entirely."

He squeezed her hand. "Exactly. So, I'd better say good night." He brushed his lips softly against hers. "Will I see you tomorrow night?"

"Yes, if you'd like."

"I'd like that very much. I'll call you tomorrow morning after I get back to the office."

The look in his eyes told her he didn't want to leave any more than she wanted him to. She stood on the porch and watched until his taillights disappeared down the street, then she went inside.

She felt the frown wrinkle across her forehead. He had done it to her again. As soon as she tried to talk to him about the company expansion plans and what type of job might be available for her, he had changed the subject. This time, however, instead of changing the topic of conversation, he had enfolded her in yet another one of his spine-tingling kisses that literally took her breath away.

Perhaps she was being too subtle and he wasn't understanding what she meant. Maybe the best thing was to come right out and tell him she wanted his help, why she needed it and exactly what she wanted to accomplish. She shook her head. She wasn't at all confident about how to proceed with her plan…or whether she should.

Angie went inside, moving quietly through the house so she wouldn't wake her brother. She undressed and climbed into bed. Even though her eyes were closed she could not turn off her thoughts, especially the new one that said Ty probably suspected what she was up to and had been diplomatically avoiding the conversation. Perhaps his teasing comment about her being an industrial spy was less tease and more serious than she had first thought.

She turned over and shoved her pillow into a different shape. Why was she feeling so troubled and unsettled? It was true that the situation had become more complicated than she had intended, especially where Ty was concerned. All she had been looking for was someone who would be fun without any pressure for her to fit into a preconceived role or a need to impress, and Tyler Farrell certainly filled those initial requirements. She laughed when they were together. She enjoyed the fun, carefree activities. Everything with him was open, easy and stress-free.

A dark cloud invaded her thoughts. Well, maybe she had not been really all that open with him. She certainly was not looking for another relationship. She just wanted to put some fun and adventure into her life and procure a position with her brother's company that would be a career rather than a job. Was that asking too much?

Had she been purposely misleading Ty? Deceiving him? Would he think she was leading him on for her own selfish purposes? The bothersome thought lingered in her mind until she finally succumbed to the need for sleep.

"Don't worry, Mac. I understand about your work schedule…honest. You stay as late as you need to. I'll be fine."

Angie quickly concluded her phone conversation with her brother. Ty would be picking her up in half an hour and she hadn't even started to get ready yet. They were going to spend the evening doing what Ty had described as barbecue and the hot tub—just a casual evening at his house. A little shiver of anticipation, combined with a hint of trepidation, immediately told her it would be a special night. She had known him as an adult for only a few days, yet she felt so comfortable and at ease with him, not to mention the undeniable intense attraction she felt toward him.

And now they would be spending the evening in the privacy of his house, just the two of them without anyone else around. The mention of the hot tub evoked a very sensual feel that left her short of breath just thinking about the possibilities. She shook her head in dismay. Ty was an incredibly sexy man, charming and lots of fun. But was she prepared to take what wasn't really a relationship, something she wasn't even looking for, to a more intimate level?

If they made love, she could no longer claim that it was only a casual thing and they weren't really involved. For Angie making love was not just a pleasant diversion. It was a serious step and one she did not take lightly. Was she prepared to admit to herself that in the short span of her adult association with him, as ridiculous as it sounded, she just might be falling in love with Tyler Farrell? That she was ready to take that all-important serious step?

Her own thoughts shocked her. Where had the word *love* come from? It certainly had not been a conscious thought. All along she had steadfastly maintained she did not want to become entrenched in another relationship. She had escaped her suffocating engagement to Caufield and was not eager to tie herself to one person again. Love and marriage were definitely not in her plans, at least not for several more years.

The realization stunned her. How had this happened? How in the world had she allowed her thoughts to set out on such a flight of fancy? There was nothing serious going on between her and Ty. They were just two friends enjoying each other's company—nothing more. She forced her concerns aside and turned her attentions toward getting ready.

She set out her swimsuit for use in the hot tub. It would be a fun night. Just a casual backyard barbecue and relaxing in the hot tub. It didn't need to have the sensual overtones she had tried to attribute to it. She stared at her reflection in the mirror, a scowl marring her features. Who was she kidding? She looked forward to spending another evening with Tyler Farrell and the thought of the hot bubbling water perfectly matched the heated anticipation bubbling through her veins.

It had all seemed harmless enough at first—the game of sexy banter, flirting, playful touches and caresses and even the tingling kisses. Ty was charming and good company. And most of all he was fun to be with. She enjoyed laughing and the carefree feelings that went with it. With Ty there was always something fun going on, so much so that it took her a while to realize she had allowed her goal of eliciting his help in convincing Mac of her job qualifications to slip from first place in her priorities. It was still what she wanted, but she had neglected putting a plan into effect. And with each kiss any sort of a plan on how to accomplish that goal seemed to slip further and further into the background.

One thing was for sure…it was no longer a matter of the two of them simply grabbing a bite to eat or enjoying a tourist attraction. Somehow they had moved from casual friendship to something much more personal. A sensual aura surrounded everything they did together, no matter how innocent the activity.

And the not-so-innocent loomed large in her mind, too. What had started with casual touches had evolved into caresses and the type of toe-curling passion she had experienced the first time Ty kissed her—a passion that burned hot inside her, fueled by a flame of desire she could not extinguish. And the desire was no longer relegated solely to the physical, either. Even though she wanted to deny it, she knew her emotions were just as involved.

She finished getting dressed, putting on a touch of lipstick just as the doorbell rang. The excitement built inside her as she rushed to answer it. The moment she opened the door his sexual magnetism flowed to her, touching her on every level of her existence. Every embrace, caress and kiss they had shared exploded in her memory, as real as when it had happened.

Ty stepped inside the house and immediately drew her into his arms. "Are you ready to journey forth?"

"Yes. I'll grab my purse and swimsuit, then we can go."

He caressed her shoulders and ran one hand down her back to her waist. "I'm not quite ready to leave yet. I have something I need to do first." A moment later his mouth was on hers.

Angie was all he had thought about the entire day— a day that seemed to drag by as he counted the hours until he would see her again. Now she was in his arms and they had the entire evening in front of them. He reluctantly broke off the kiss, then took a calming breath as an uneasy feeling rose inside him.

"We'd better stop doing this…at least for the time being. I think Mac is on his way home." His own words caught him by surprise. A quick jolt of guilt told him how unsettled he was in his mind about his pursuit of Angie, what his true intentions were and what the ultimate impact on his relationship with Mac would be.

"Really? I talked to him a little while ago and he said he wouldn't be home for dinner because he still had a lot of work to do."

"That was before someone carrying a nearly full pot of coffee rounded a corner and ran into him." Ty attempted without success to stop the chuckle as he recalled the collision. "Mac, of course, didn't find it as amusing as I did. Coffee on the walls," he gestured with a wave of his hand indicating a large expanse of space, "coffee on the floor and coffee all over a very unhappy McConnor Coleman."

Her laugh joined his. "I'll bet that was quite a sight. Mac hates being dirty and messy. He's been that way for as long as I can remember."

"The last I saw of him was his back as he retreated down the hall toward his office muttering something about needing to go home to change clothes and that was about ten minutes ago. So, he could be here any minute."

"You're right. We wouldn't want him to catch us." Her gaze locked with his for a hot moment, sending a wave of desire coursing through her. Her words turned husky surrounded by a breathless quality. "Not that we're doing anything wrong."

"True…" He reached out and brushed his fingertips across her cheek and tucked an errant lock of hair behind her ear. He skimmed his fingers down the side of her neck until they came to rest on her shoulder. "We're not doing anything wrong." The words only reinforced what he knew but didn't want to admit, that he had less than honorable designs on the forbidden temptation standing in front of him. A definite internal conflict pulled him in two directions. On one hand was his desire for Angie and on the other his loyalty to Mac.

And on top of that was his confusion over exactly what his true intentions were. The one thing he did know was that he had somehow gotten in over his head where Angie was concerned. He knew he couldn't continue to tread water. He had to do something, but he didn't know what.

Ty recovered from his moment of confusion by pushing his thoughts aside. He had the scene all set at his house. They would grill some chicken on the deck, then enjoy champagne in the hot tub. It would be an evening devoted to sensual pleasure.

Angie gathered her purse and swimsuit and they left just as Mac pulled into the driveway. As he climbed out of his car, his gaze darted from Ty to Angie and back to Ty.

There was an uneasiness in Mac's voice, a forced casualness. "You two going out again tonight? That's every night this week." Mac turned his attention to Ty. "It's nice of you to keep Angie company so I can finish the design. I know what a busy social life you lead. I hope she isn't taking too much of your time."

"Don't worry about us. We both know how important the design project is and the time crunch you have." Ty placed his hand at the small of Angie's back and gently pressed to start her walking toward his car. "Tonight we're going to a barbecue."

A look of surprise darted across Mac's face. "A barbecue?"

"Yes...and we're running late." Ty indicated the front of Mac's shirt. He tried without success to hold back a teasing grin. "You seem to have had a little accident. Did anyone get hurt or was your shirt the only casualty?"

Mac acknowledged the large stain on his shirt, but scowled at Ty's ill-timed attempt at humor. "I'm only home long enough to get a clean shirt."

Ty flashed an outgoing smile as he turned toward the street. "We'll be running along. See you later."

"Don't wait up." She hadn't meant anything by it, but Angie regretted saying the words as soon as they were out of her mouth. The expression that quickly clouded Mac's features told her he had interpreted them in an entirely different manner than she intended.

Ty hurried her to his car and a minute later they were on the way to his house. A little pang of guilt pushed at him. He had purposely deceived Mac in not telling him that the barbecue was at his house and then he had hurried away before Mac could question him about his plans. He didn't like the feeling of sneaking around behind Mac's back even though that wasn't what he was doing—at least not really.

Confusion raced through him, increasing to a new level each time he was with Angie. The warning look on Mac's face and the protective edge to his voice every time he referred to her as his kid sister continued to play through his mind. Yet the person he had become very attached to in such a short time was a delightful and enchanting woman who could in no way be thought of merely as someone's *kid sister*.

They drove along in silence, each seemingly preoccupied by personal thoughts. Ty also lived on Bainbridge Island, only about a ten minute drive from Mac's house. He pulled his car into the garage and they entered the house through the kitchen. Angie set her purse and swimsuit on the table.

He brushed a quick kiss against her lips. "I've had chicken in the refrigerator marinating in a special barbecue sauce all day long. I'll get the charcoal started, then we can have a glass of wine while the chicken cooks."

"Is there something I can do to help? Do you want me to make the salad?"

"That would be nice, thank you. You'll find what you need in the refrigerator. I'll be right back."

Angie found the lettuce, tomatoes and a few other ingredients and set about making a tossed salad. Ty lit the charcoal, then retrieved a bottle of white wine from the wine rack and put it into the wine chiller.

They were soon enjoying a delicious dinner out on the deck, the cool night air warmed by the blaze in the outdoor fireplace. The conversation was light, but underneath sizzled a layer of sexual tension enhanced by the bubbling of the hot tub about ten feet away. It was a sound that beckoned, a sound that promised untold pleasure. A sound that soon filled the air with a sensual rhythm that resonated to the very core of their being and touched the most primal of desires.

After dinner Angie helped him carry the dishes into the kitchen. When she started to rinse them off to put them in the dishwasher, Ty stopped her. His voice contained a huskiness that sent a little tingle of excitement up her spine.

He kissed the side of her neck, then whispered in her ear. "I can do that later. Why don't you change into your swimsuit while I change into mine and we'll settle into the hot tub."

It was the moment she had anticipated yet at the same time had been apprehensive about. Would they make love that night? The possibility heated her yearnings while at the same time filling her with uncertainty. She found the prospect of becoming intimate with Tyler Farrell a little bit intimidating.

Regardless of what her brother chose to believe, she had not spent her adult years cloistered away from life, although she knew her experience was less than that of the women Ty dated. Would she be a disappointment to him? If she suddenly rebuffed his advances after allowing the passionate kisses and the tender caresses, would he think she was nothing more than a tease? Someone just leading him on in some sort of adolescent game?

A little tremor of anxiety accompanied her words as she picked up her swimsuit. ''I'll be right back.''

Angie changed and appeared on the deck a few minutes later. Ty was already there. A solid jolt of lust swept through her senses when she saw him dressed only in his swimsuit. His long tanned legs, broad shoulders and hard chest were certainly enough to turn the head of any woman. He was the most perfect specimen of male physique she had ever seen. Her breathing quickened and her mouth went dry. She may have been uncertain a few minutes ago, but that had all changed in the twinkling of an eye. Or more accurately, the devilish gleam in Ty's hazel eyes.

He flashed a dazzling smile as he blatantly did a visual trace of every line and curve she possessed. The two-piece red swimsuit revealed a body that would send any man's senses skyrocketing. The heat churned low inside him as the blood rushed hot and fast through his veins. ''You...in that swimsuit...'' His voice contained a huskiness he couldn't hide. ''That's a sight that could make grown men tremble.'' And he was no exception.

''Thank you.'' The crimson tinge of embarrassment spread across her cheeks and forehead.

He held out his hand to her, but noticed the moment's hesitation before she took it. She was not the only one filled with uncertainty. He had set up dinner and an evening that screamed seduction and could only lead to sensual pleasure. But suddenly he was very unsure of himself. He didn't know how to proceed, or whether he should proceed at all. To say he felt reticent would be an understatement of monumental proportions. He knew exactly what he wanted, but his loyalty to Mac continued to play havoc with his conscience.

He was torn. He suspected he was too involved as far as keeping an emotional distance from her was concerned. Suspected...that was a laugh. He didn't suspect—he *knew*.

They settled into the steamy swirl of the hot tub. He watched, nearly mesmerized, as the water bubbled along the edge of her swimsuit top, tickled the exposed portion of her breasts and dived into her cleavage. He wanted to follow the trail of bubbles, to know the intimate recess hidden in the crevasse of the red fabric. He wanted to know the feel of her bare skin against his, to succumb to the swirling heat of the water, to spend the rest of the night making passionate love to this enticing woman.

He fought to clear his mind of the delicious possibilities. He pulled the bottle from the ice bucket and poured each of them a glass of champagne. He held out his glass toward her. "To a very lovely lady, one who excites my senses."

"Thank you."

He saw the flush spread across her cheeks again. Had he said too much? Admitted more than he should have? Allowed a hint of his erotic thoughts and desires to escape into the open? He closed his eyes for a second in an attempt to gather his composure before he did something he knew he shouldn't.

It didn't help. The pull of the irresistible force was too strong—his ability to resist too weak.

He slid over next to her and gathered her into his arms. A moment later his mouth found hers and all the underlying sexual tension exploded into reality. Wet skin against wet skin with only the tiniest amount of swimsuit fabric preventing them from joining together as one. He twined his tongue with hers while slowly tugging on the strap tied at her back. The strap gave way. Then he tugged on the tie at her nape. The top of her swimsuit fell to the water, revealing her bare breasts.

Her puckered nipples appeared then disappeared in the foamy swirl of water. A sudden shortness of breath caught in his lungs, leaving him gasping for air. He wanted to touch her, to caress the perfect roundness of her breasts, to taste them. Then the image of Mac's disapproval and his protective tone of voice again invaded Ty's consciousness. Did he dare pursue what he wanted? And if he did, what might the consequences be?

A moment later his mouth was on hers again. No more thoughts, no more concerns. She was far too tempting and he wanted her way too much. One lingering thought tried to remain in the forefront, the one that asked what his true feelings were. Just how emotionally involved had he become even though he didn't want to be?

His tongue meshed with hers sending a wave of exhilaration through Angie's body. The hot water swirled around her bare breasts, keeping her nerve endings primed and ready for more…much more. When he had tugged on her swimsuit strap she knew the time for a decision could not be put off any longer. She needed to either stop what was happening or welcome it with open arms. Her breathing increased and her pulse raced. The steam rose into the cool night air, enclosing them in a diaphanous cocoon of sensuality.

She totally let go of her inhibitions and allowed her

body and senses to flow with the dynamic energy of Tyler Farrell. She had earlier suspected she might be falling in love with him. Now she was becoming more convinced of it even though she didn't want it to be true. Was it too late to stop this falling-in-love process? To turn back the hands of time? Could she persuade herself that it was only lust? Physical desire for a very attractive and sexy man and nothing more? What would the consequences be if they made love? Was it something she could handle and keep under control so that it didn't become more than she wanted it to be? Too many questions—and no answers anywhere in sight.

All her thoughts stopped the moment his hand caressed her breast, then cupped the fullness. Any composure she might have been clinging to quickly evaporated. The warmth of his touch made even the temperature of the bubbling water seem cool by comparison. She skimmed her fingers across the wet skin of his back, each touch sending another ripple of excitement coursing through her veins. She felt herself slipping further and further away from reality as she moved into the world of pleasure and total delight.

He pulled her onto his lap. Being enfolded in his arms while surrounded by the swirling clouds of steam heightened her already stimulated senses. His growing arousal pressed against her thigh. The situation had moved rapidly beyond the point where she would be able to easily put a stop to it—if it wasn't already too late.

A soft moan escaped her throat as his lips nibbled at the corner of her mouth, moved down the side of her neck and across her shoulder, leaving sizzling trails of pleasure. Then he moved lower until he reached her breast. Excitement rippled through her body. Her head jerked backward as he teased her nipple with his tongue until it formed a taut peak. He drew the puckered treat into his mouth, sending a quick jolt of exhilaration racing through her. Her breathing became ragged. Every tautly drawn nerve ending tingled with anticipation—and also an ever-increasing level of apprehension.

Four

A cloud of trepidation and doubt settled over Angie. Ty was so smooth and experienced. Everything about him excited her in ways she hadn't dreamed possible. But was it as Mac had said? That Ty lived in the fast lane and she wasn't in his league? The insecurities she had learned to hide from everyone else now forced their way to the front. Her internal battle raged at full force. She fought to bring her rampaging desires under control and regain her composure. She had to put a stop to what was happening before it was too late. Her words came out as a breathless whisper—part anticipation, part regret and all enveloped in the anxiety she couldn't control.

"Ty...we can't..."

Her voice floated toward him through a swirling cloud of steam and euphoria, the words barely discernible above the sound of the bubbling water. The meaning of those words took a few moments to register with him. He tried to pull in a calming breath and force some sort of rational thought. He had never wanted anyone as much in his life as he did Angie Coleman at that moment.

"Can't?" His voice was as breathless as hers and conveyed his confusion mixed with a heavy dose of frustration.

"Why not?" He tilted his head back just enough to be able to see her face.

He expected to see the glow of excitement shining in the depths of her eyes. Judging by the ever-increasing passion surrounding the many kisses they had shared and her enthusiastic response to his advances, he had anticipated finding a level of desire to match his own. What he caught sight of instead was a wariness and uncertainty that jerked his senses to attention as if someone had thrown cold water on his escalating arousal.

He held her in his arms as his mood shifted from lustful craving to reassurance and caring. It was an odd transition, one he had never before experienced. He took several deep breaths in order to bring his ragged breathing under control and curtail his heightened desires. He wasn't sure what had just happened. He knew he didn't want to turn loose of her. He continued to hold her in his arms and cherish the closeness of the moment.

"I thought you also wanted...well..." He took another calming breath. He knew he needed to be very careful in the words he chose. "I'm sorry, Angie." He pulled her tighter into his embrace, not at all sure he was doing the right thing. "I didn't realize I was pushing you into something you didn't want—"

She placed her fingertips against his lips to still his words. "Maybe *not yet* would be a more accurate way of saying it." She wasn't sure exactly what she did want, but she knew she didn't want him to think the door had been closed permanently. But first she needed to clear the confusion whirling around inside her.

A sense of relief flooded through her as he pressed his lips against her forehead. Not only had he accepted her decision without challenging it, he had not pulled away from her or made her feel as if his only interest in her was sex. It felt so right being in his arms. Another moment of doubt clouded her thoughts. Perhaps it was too comfortable, too much the way she would like it always to be rather than a reflection of reality.

The disturbing thought lingered in her mind. Falling in love with someone, especially someone like Tyler Farrell, was not part of her plan. It probably wasn't a good idea even if she didn't already have an agenda for her future. He was the type of man who would not allow himself to be trapped in a relationship. Her thoughts startled her. A relationship…she had just escaped from a relationship where she felt trapped. That was certainly a direction she didn't want to go again. She needed to refocus her efforts on her career goals and keep that foremost in her mind.

Her attention wrenched back to the present when his hand grazed the side of her bare breast. Just the slightest intimate contact and her desires burst into flame again. She had to put some physical distance between herself and Ty or the next step she took would be toward his bedroom. But before she could react, Ty eased her off his lap and onto the bench seat in the hot tub. Then he fished the top of her swimsuit from the swirling water and handed it to her.

His breathing might have been under control, but his husky words were surrounded by the emotions and desires that continued to fill every corner of his consciousness. "I think it might be better for both of us if you put this back on."

She took the piece of clothing from him. "Yes, you're right."

Ty's action of turning away to give her privacy while she adjusted the top of her swimsuit was not lost on Angie. The gentlemanly gesture was certainly not the type of behavior associated with a callous womanizer who had only one thing on his mind. A soft glow filled her with a tender warmth. The heated lust of moments ago had transformed into a sense of closeness. She had never been enveloped in such a total feeling of caring with Caufield, never felt the type of tenderness and warmth she felt with Ty.

The overwhelming sensation frightened her in both its hidden meanings and blatant assault on her emotions leaving her totally confused about what the future held. She knew what she wanted—a position of responsibility in her brother's company, something that would be a career for her. At least she thought she knew. She had made a plan and put it into action. Now she wasn't sure any longer. And the confusing factor that had been added to the equation was the very disconcerting presence of Tyler Farrell. He scared her—not physically, but most assuredly on an emotional level.

Ty handed her a filled glass and offered a reassuring smile. "We can still enjoy the hot tub and some champagne, can't we?" He noticed the slight tremble of his hand telling him how stimulated he still was despite the fact that he knew any possibility of making love that evening was gone. Hopefully she wouldn't notice it. The last thing he wanted was to make her more uncomfortable than she apparently already was.

She accepted the champagne and returned his smile. "Of course."

He clinked his glass against hers, then took a sip. He eyed her carefully as she took a drink. She appeared composed on the outside, but he could see the anxiety and uncertainty in the depths of her eyes. He looked around at the scene he had staged—champagne, a bubbling hot tub, swimsuits which were the minimum amount of clothes they could be wearing and still be wearing something. It was a carefully prepared setting that screamed seduction and a night of passionate love-making.

He had invited her to his lair knowing exactly where he expected the night to go. He had used it many times, but always on very willing partners. Angie was not like other women, certainly not like the many women he dated and bedded. His sidetracked seduction attempt pulled at his emotions while inflicting feelings of guilt.

They stayed in the hot tub for half an hour, sipping champagne and valiantly attempting to ignore the sensual swirl enveloping them in desire while carrying on a casual conversation. And with each passing minute Angie became less sure about having put a stop to what had happened and more certain that making love with Ty would be ecstasy beyond anything she had ever known.

And all of her conflicting thoughts and feelings said one thing to her—she had to get safely away from Tyler Farrell. She needed to clear her mind and think things through without the distraction of this incredibly desirable man.

Angie set her empty glass aside and rose to her feet.

She picked up a large towel and began to pat the water from her skin. "It's getting late. I think I'd better start for home. Between the champagne and the therapeutic effect of the hot tub, I'm so relaxed I can barely keep my eyes open." She offered what she hoped was an engaging smile rather than one filled with anxiety.

He climbed out of the hot tub and grabbed a towel. "Of course. I'll change into some dry clothes and drive you back to Mac's house." He paused a moment, then pulled her gently into his arms. He held her tenderly in his embrace without being aggressive. He cradled her head against his shoulder. He searched for the proper words, something that would put her at ease yet allow him to know how things stood between them.

His words were more hesitant than he wanted them to be. "I...I hope my actions haven't put a strain on our seeing each other again." He cupped her face in his hands and peered into the depths of her eyes. He placed a soft kiss on her lips, nothing too intimate and definitely not demanding. "I truly didn't mean to make you uncomfortable."

A shy smile turned the corners of her mouth. "Nothing has changed. I would be very disappointed if we didn't continue to see each other."

Angie knew it was her fault. She had given him the green light with her actions, then changed her mind and pulled back. Yet he was the one accepting responsibility. It was certainly a gracious gesture, not that of a callous playboy. And it intensified the rapidly growing emotional attachment she felt for him. Did she dare allow the word *love* to once again be a part of her thoughts where Ty was concerned? A little shiver of anxiety made its way across her skin.

She tried to lighten the moment. "The air is a little

chilly. We'd better get into some dry clothes before we both end up with a cold."

She retreated to the guest bathroom to change while he did the same in his bedroom. Then he drove her back to Mac's house.

Ty held her hand as they walked up the path toward the front door. "May I see you tomorrow night? Maybe dinner and a movie, or whatever you'd like to do? I know Mac will still be working on the design project. He's not happy with the way it's going and has redone some portions of it. That's one of the reasons it's taking him so long."

"I read in the newspaper this morning about a new art gallery in Seattle. There's going to be a grand opening tomorrow night. Perhaps we could attend?"

"That sounds great. I'll pick you up at six o'clock so that we can make the six forty-five ferry."

She gave his hand a little squeeze. "I'll see you then."

She watched until his taillights disappeared around the corner, then went inside. It had been a profound evening, one that had helped crystallize some of her emotions but had left her very unsettled in other areas. His actions following her decision not to make love had been commendable and showed a great deal of consideration for her wishes regardless of his personal desires.

And it made her feel that much closer to him on all levels.

Pangs of regret over her decision to call a halt to things had already started to filter through to her conscious thoughts. Now she wondered what tomorrow night would bring. She slid into bed and closed her eyes. Vivid images of Tyler Farrell danced through her mind along with the heated desire that still coursed through her veins.

The next evening, Ty rang the bell and a moment later Angie opened the front door. He immediately stepped into the entryway. "I'm sorry I'm late."

"That's okay."

He glanced at his watch as he shook his head in irritation. "I got stuck at the office in a meeting. I didn't call because I kept thinking I'd be able to leave any minute and now it's too late to catch the six-forty-five ferry to Seattle."

"We can catch the next one."

He pulled her into his arms, being careful not to hold her too tight but unable to resist taking the action. "I'm afraid by the time we do that we'll end up being too late to attend the gallery opening." He looked at her questioningly, as if he wasn't sure what to say. "Maybe we can go tomorrow night instead? We'll miss the opening festivities, champagne and hors d'oeuvres, but it won't be as crowded."

She smiled in response to his obvious uncertainty. "I'd like that very much."

"In the meantime, we can still go out and get something to eat. How about the pub at the waterfront where we first had lunch?" He glanced down at what he was wearing, then extended a sheepish smile. "I had to dress appropriately for my meeting. Since we aren't going to the gallery opening, I'd really like to get out of this suit and tie and into something comfortable before we do anything else."

"Same here. If you give me a couple of minutes, I'd like to change clothes, too."

"I'll wait right here."

Angie made a quick change from the dress she had been wearing to a pair of slacks and simple pullover top. They drove to Ty's house where he excused himself and went to his bedroom to change clothes.

His absence gave her an opportunity to study the surroundings he had chosen for himself, something she had not been able to do the previous night. The expensive furnishings and decoration reflected the good taste of the owner—elegant yet comfortable and inviting. She examined several porcelain objects inside a glass-fronted cabinet. From a distance they appeared to be delicate statuettes. Up close she discovered the whimsy and humor the figurines projected. Another indication of the fun-loving personality of the owner.

She studied the titles of the books that filled several bookcases. They contained just about every genre of fiction, biographies and autobiographies, research books on various topics and general nonfiction. It was an impressive collection of reading material covering a wide range of topics.

She wandered toward the large window that looked out to the deck, the private dock and the ocean beyond. She closed her eyes and allowed the tantalizing sensations of the previous night to wash through her body. Her nerve endings came alive, every desire she had experienced in the hot tub once again playing havoc with her senses. Her mind drifted to where things had been headed when she put a stop to it. A huff of regret spilled out from her throat. *Chickened out* was a more accurate description. She had allowed her insecurities to dictate her actions.

Her thoughts came to a screeching halt when his arms slipped around her waist from behind and he pulled her to him until her back rested against his chest. His smooth masculine voice whispered in her ear, sending a tingle of excitement rippling across her skin.

"A penny for your thoughts." He leaned his head over her shoulder and placed a tender kiss on her cheek. "You looked like you were a million miles away. Anything you'd care to share?"

She placed her hands on top of his, the physical contact completing the feeling of comfort and caring that radiated from him. "My mind was kind of wandering…just thinking about what might—" She cut off her own words. She had said more than she intended.

"About what might…?" He turned her around until she faced him. He placed his fingertips under her chin and lifted until he could look into her eyes. The wariness and uncertainty of the night before had vanished. He tried to read her thoughts, determine what had been going through her mind. He didn't want to make another mistake by taking too much for granted. But that did not stop the heated desire pushing at his consciousness, reminding him how much he wanted her.

"Were you thinking about what might have happened if things had moved to their logical conclusion last night?" He ran his fingers through her silky hair, caressed her shoulders, then held her close.

"Angie…" He felt her arms encircle his waist. He pulled her body tighter against his. "I want so much to make love to you, but I don't want to rush things." He kissed her tenderly. "I want it to be something you want as much as I do."

"What about Mac?" She wasn't sure why those words had escaped her mouth, but they had. It was testimony to her ingrained concern about her brother's opinion, but at what cost?

A slight grin tugged at the corners of his mouth. ''I like Mac very much, but he's not my type. He's not the one I want to make love to.'' The grin disappeared and his expression became very serious. ''Mac is your brother and he's my business partner and best friend, but this doesn't involve him. This is something between you and me and no one else.''

''You're right.'' She had allowed her fears to dictate to her last night when they were in the hot tub. She would not make the same mistake tonight. A moment of doubt tried to cloud her thoughts. At least she hoped her decision wasn't going to turn out to be a mistake. She reached her face up to his until their lips touched.

The moment her mouth came in contact with his a jolt of electricity surged through his body. His hand slid down her back and came to rest on the curve of her bottom. He snuggled her hips up against his as his tongue meshed with hers. He reveled in the sensuality of the texture. If he lived to be a hundred years old he would never have enough of her taste.

Ty scooped her up in his arms and carried her across the house to his bedroom. He placed her on his king-size bed, then quickly kicked off his shoes. He yanked off his sweater and tossed it on the chair. Then he was next to her, stroking her hair and placing soft kisses on her face. ''Are you sure you're okay with this? I don't want to cause you any problems or make you feel like you were being coerced into something you didn't really want.''

''Yes...I'm sure.'' And she was. No feelings of guilt and no doubts. She wiggled her feet out of her shoes and let them drop to the floor. It felt right. Making love with Tyler Farrell was exactly what she wanted. A glimmer of a thought tried to pierce her consciousness, asking her how much more she wanted, but she refused to acknowledge the concern.

A moment later she found herself enfolded in Ty's arms. His mouth captured hers in an incendiary kiss, demanding from her yet giving everything all at the same time. She lost herself in his tantalizing touch and earth-moving kisses. Her ragged breathing matched the pounding of her heart. The heat flowed through her veins touching every part of her body.

If his kisses were a portent of what making love with Ty would be like, then she knew she was about to experience something very profound and special. She welcomed his tongue as it twined with hers. She ran her hands across the bare skin of his back, his well-muscled torso rippling beneath her fingers.

Her touch was so light that it almost tickled before fanning the flames of his desires. She was so exquisite, so breathtaking…so perfect. His chest heaved with his labored breathing. He ran his fingers through her hair as his kiss deepened, then he slipped his hands under her shirt. He wanted the barrier of her clothes out of the way. He craved the feel of her bare skin against his, to be able to touch her everywhere, to know every intimate place, to know what excited her. He wanted to both experience and share her pleasure.

His hardened arousal strained against the front of his jeans. As much as he wanted to divest himself of the rest of his clothes, he didn't want to let go of her, to break that physical contact that so inflamed his senses. He pulled her shirt over her head and tossed it on the chair with his sweater. When he reached for the waistband of his jeans, his fingers met hers. His words came out in a husky whisper.

"Need to get these off…and your clothes…"

Her words were equally ragged. "Yes...I'll do this."

Each quickly removed their own remaining pieces of clothing, then fell back on the bed into each other's arms. Ty ran his hands down the length of her torso, reveling in the creamy smoothness of her skin. With all the women he had made love to over the years, never had he experienced anything quite like the sensation of her bare body pressed against his. He wanted all of her and he wanted it right now. And at the same time he also wanted to take it slow and make the evening last forever.

Again his tongue twined with hers as he cupped the fullness of her breast in his hand. Her tautly puckered nipple pressed into his palm. He smothered her face with feverish kisses, tasting her skin as he moved down her body. He teased her other nipple with his tongue before drawing it into his mouth. No one had ever excited him the way she did. Just touching her sent waves of yearning crashing through his body.

He trailed his fingers across her abdomen, then through the downy softness nestled at the apex of her thighs. He inserted his finger into the moist heat. Her quick intake of breath and soft moan of delight fueled his desires. His pulse raced. His mouth captured hers with a demanding fervor.

Angie's mind swirled in a sensual fog of euphoria. His mouth gave as much as it demanded. His body shuddered as she stroked his hardness, then wrapped her hand around his manhood. He pressed his hand against her intimate core, his fingers working magic. Levels of pleasure built one on top of the other deep inside her until they reached a crescendo peak. The convulsions reached out to every part of her body, filling her with total ecstasy.

He knew he could not wait any longer. He saw the passion that covered her features and glowed in the depths of her eyes. It matched the desire burning inside him. With a slightly trembling hand he reached for the drawer of the nightstand and took out the condom packet. A minute later he nestled his body between her legs, his hardened arousal slowly penetrating the core of her heat.

A searing jolt of pure rapture swept through his body as the folds of her femininity closed in around his manhood, encasing him in a tight cocoon. The sensation had his senses reeling, leaving him nearly breathless. He gulped in a lungful of air and set a slow rhythm that quickly escalated as his excitement grew.

Angie tightened her arms and legs around his body. She had never experienced anything like the passion of Tyler Farrell. Every place he touched her left her craving more of his magic. She arched her hips upward to meet each of his downward thrusts. Their bodies moved in unity, each so attuned to the other. It was as if they had been making love together for all their adult lives. She had never felt so at one with another human being. Every movement…every breath…every conscious moment flowed and swirled into an ethereal oneness that left her wanting more and more.

The pace quickened as did her heartbeat and breathing. Wave after wave of euphoria rippled through her, then a sizzling arc of electricity shot through her body. Her head jerked back into the pillow as the final rapture convulsed deep inside her. She clung to him as if he were the center of her life, the main focus around which her very existence revolved.

Ty's heart pounded in his chest. The moment she tightened her arms around him he shuddered with release, the hard spasms moving up into his chest and down through his thighs. He held her tightly until the spasms subsided and he had regained some control of his ragged breathing. If only he could force some sort of control over his emotions, to be able to think of it as just another night of passionate fun and games with a very willing and sexy partner. But as much as he wanted to be able to do that, he couldn't. There was no way he could think of Angie in the same category as any of the other women he had ever dated.

There was something so very special about her. It was the same something that frightened him so much. He placed a soft kiss on her forehead, hoping it would somehow calm the inner anxiety that threatened to take over.

He stroked her hair, kissed her forehead again and continued to hold her in his embrace. The physical aspects of their lovemaking may have quieted, but the emotional turmoil had just begun. It twisted inside him, telling him exactly what he didn't want to know—that he was more than just physically involved with her. But how much more? It was a question that scared him. What would she be expecting from him? What kind of relationship did she think they had? And equally important, what was he willing to give? It was a question that preyed on his mind, one for which he did not have an answer…yet.

An answer he wasn't sure he was ready to find.

Five

Ty dropped another kiss on Angie's forehead. "Are you okay?" He tried to control the emotion in his voice, but without much success. "Is there anything I can get for you?"

She snuggled into his embrace. "I'm fine." Fine? She was more than fine. She had certainly made love before. She was far from promiscuous, but she had experienced more partners than just her ex-fiancé. But nowhere in her life had she encountered anything like the pure heated sexual magnetism of Tyler Farrell.

Before that night she had only suspected she might be falling in love with him. Now that uncertainty was rapidly fading to be replaced by emotions she could no longer deny but was not ready to fully accept. She remained still with her eyes closed as she savored the comfort of his arms and the warm glow of contentment. She tried to keep the smile from turning the corners of her mouth as she allowed thoughts of what the future held.

Suddenly her warm glow grew dim as a cloud of doubt appeared on the horizon. The dark cloud tried to invade her euphoria. She didn't have the slightest idea what Ty felt or what he wanted. Was she nothing more than just another of the many women he dated? Just another conquest, as Mac had tried to tell her?

She fought off the potentially crippling doubt by reminding herself of her original goal and plan. She was not looking for a relationship. She had other things she wanted to do with her life first. And even if she was looking for a relationship, did she really think a man like Tyler Farrell would be the type to make a commitment?

She reaffirmed her determination to pursue her goal. She wanted to earn Mac's approval and his respect for her abilities as an adult. She wanted to secure her own future through her own efforts without Mac giving her a job just because she asked. It was very important to her to be able to stand on her own feet and earn her own way. She remained in Ty's arms, lost in her own thoughts about what the future held and where she was going. A future that may or may not include Tyler Farrell.

She turned to glance at the clock on the nightstand. It was still early. It had been only a little after seven o'clock when they had made their way to the bedroom.

"Is something wrong?" He immediately sat up, drawing her body tightly to him. His gaze quickly shot around the room, trying to find what had grabbed her attention. "What do you need? What can I do?" They were questions that had a far deeper meaning than what the present circumstances would dictate. Making love

to Angie had a far greater impact on him than he had
ever imagined it could. And it had left him reeling with
uncertainty and confusion. If only he could figure out
where they stood, what the future held and what he
wanted.

"I was just wondering what time it was."

He sank back into the warmth of the bed, taking her
with him. He stroked her hair and reveled in the tender
closeness. Exactly what were his true feelings toward
her? It was a loaded question, one with an answer that
scared him right down to his toes. A committed relationship was not for him. He had watched his parents'
marriage disintegrate into bitter arguments and at best
nothing more than strained attempts to politely tolerate
each other. He had been that route with his own marriage. There was no way he would ever allow himself
to be suckered into a commitment to a relationship
again, regardless of how attractive it might seem at the
moment. If what two people had was right, it didn't
require words of commitment.

Yet he couldn't imagine his life without Angie being
a part of it. And it was that knowledge that tore at him,
leaving him without a clear-cut path to follow or any
solution for his inner turmoil.

And then there was Mac. He couldn't get the image
of Mac's look of disapproval out of his mind. Did Mac
truly believe that he wasn't good enough for Angie? If
so, what did that say about their friendship and business partnership? It left him as much in the dark about
how to approach things with Mac as it did in trying to
figure what he and Angie had together.

Ty placed a soft kiss on Angie's cheek. "It's still
early and I owe you a dinner. Would you like to go to
the pub as we originally planned—" he pulled her

body tighter against his ''—or would you like to stay here and take your chances on what's in my refrigerator?''

''I'd just as soon stay here, if that's all right with you.''

''Me, too.'' He reluctantly released her from his embrace. ''Let me see if I can find something comfortable for you to put on while we putter around the kitchen.''

Ty climbed out of bed, disappeared into his bathroom, then returned a couple of minutes later. He pulled on a pair of sweatpants, then grabbed a large football jersey from a dresser drawer and handed it to her. ''Here...try this.''

She pulled the jersey on over her head, then slid out of bed. When she stood up the jersey came halfway down her thighs. ''Yes, this will be fine.''

He started to turn toward the door, but quickly whirled around and grabbed her in his arms. The spontaneous gesture was partly a need to reestablish physical contact and partly a desire to share the lingering warmth of their lovemaking that continued to permeate the air. Is this how it was going to be? His life wouldn't be complete unless he could hold her...touch her...be with her?

He lowered his mouth to hers in a tender and loving kiss, far different from the frenzied urgency of earlier. It contained warmth and caring, the type of closeness that had a feeling of permanency about it. The sensation was wonderful and comfortable. But was it too comfortable? It was a serious dilemma, one that he knew could cost him many sleepless nights and would not be easily resolved.

Angie wound her arms around his waist. He made her feel so special. It was a feeling she didn't want to ever lose. But at what cost? A little shudder of apprehension swept through her. What had she gotten herself into? What happened to her decision to not become involved with anyone?

Ty's kiss deepened, sweeping away all her doubts and concerns in a heated heartbeat. He pulled her body tightly against his, then skimmed his hands under the bottom of the football jersey and up the smooth skin of her thighs. He cupped the roundness of her bare bottom and pulled her hips against his. His rapidly hardening manhood pressed against her, igniting her own simmering desires. Dinner be damned...she wanted Tyler Farrell. He was all the sustenance she needed.

He scooped her up in his arms. A moment later they sank back into the softness of his king-size bed. Arms and legs tangled together. Mouths and tongues teased and tasted. The passion they had earlier shared burst once again into an all-consuming flame.

Ty arrived for work early the next morning. He had never felt as light of step or happy with life in general. His only regret was that Angie had not been able to spend the entire night at his house. They had agreed that it would not be a wise thing to do. He had reluctantly taken her back to Mac's house about two o'clock that morning. Even though he had not gotten more than a few hours of sleep, he felt terrific.

As soon as he turned down the hall he spotted Mac leaning against the doorjamb of his office. The expression on Mac's face struck him as intense and odd, not the usual look that said his mind was a million miles away working on some design problem.

Ty extended a pleasant smile. "Good morning, Mac.

Bright, beautiful sunny day out there and all's right with the world. How's the design project coming along?''

''I'm almost done with it. Just another day or two at the most.'' Mac shifted his weight from one foot to the other, his awkward manner testifying to his discomfort. ''Do you have a minute, Ty? There's something we need to talk about.''

Ty furrowed his brow in momentary confusion. Something was definitely bothering Mac. Could it be a business problem he wasn't aware of? Trouble with a vendor or a client? ''Sure, Mac.''

The two men entered Mac's office with Mac closing the door behind them.

Ty cocked his head and shot his partner a questioning look. ''What's up? Is there a problem?'' He watched as Mac nervously rearranged the items on his desk. A sinking feeling settled inside him, a sensation that told him this was something personal rather than business. And that could only mean one thing—Angie. His mind filled with hundreds of images of her and memories of a night of passion he knew he would never be able to duplicate with anyone else—nor did he have any desire to try. Whether he wanted it or not, she had become as much a part of his life as breathing.

Ty attempted to make light of what he suspected was about to be an unpleasant situation. He forced what he hoped sounded like a casual laugh. ''Are we on the verge of bankruptcy? Have all our employees decided to go out on strike? I didn't notice any picket signs when I came in.'' The discomfort welled inside him and his words carried an edge of irritation. ''Whatever it is, Mac, don't keep me in suspense. Just say it.''

"Yes…all right." Mac nervously cleared his throat. "It's…uh…it's about Angie."

Something in Mac's tone of voice grabbed Ty's attention. He straightened as a cold fear shot through his body. "Is she all right? Did something happen to her?"

"No, nothing like that."

Ty eyed him cautiously, not sure he really wanted to hear what Mac had to say. "Then what?"

"Well, as you know this design project has had me chained to my office for the past couple of weeks, even before Angie arrived." Mac took a swallow from his coffee cup. "And I know I asked you if you would mind entertaining her that first day she was in town."

"I believe *take her off my hands* was the way you phrased it."

"Uh…yes, well…I know how busy you are and I've been concerned about how much of your time Angie has taken up. So…I just wanted to let you know that you don't need to entertain her any longer. I'm close enough to completion on the design that I can have dinner with her in the evenings, so you don't need to put your own social life on hold any longer. I can take it from here and you can return to your many lady friends." Mac extended a smile, but it looked more nervous than sincere.

Ty bristled inside at the barely veiled insinuation that Mac was unhappy with how much time he and Angie had been spending together. He also didn't like the reference Mac had made to his *many lady friends* as if he was a blatant womanizer. It sounded as if Mac didn't want him to see Angie anymore. It was the moment he had been concerned about. Was he going to have to make a choice between his feelings for Angie and his personal and business relationship with Mac?

Would he have to sacrifice his relationship with Angie in order to preserve the company?

The dilemma presented itself as a double-edged sword. If he was forced to make a decision it wouldn't matter which side he chose because either way he would lose something special and important to him. He took a calming breath. Maybe it was his own fears that were directing his thoughts. He didn't want to jump to a wrong conclusion about what Mac really meant.

He drew in another steadying breath, held it for a moment, then slowly exhaled. He leveled a serious look at Mac and carefully measured his words. "What exactly are you saying? Are you telling me you don't want me to see Angie anymore? Have you even bothered to discuss this with her or are you making this decision for her according to what you think she should be doing?"

"Be reasonable, Ty. Angie is a young and very impressionable girl. She's not at all the type of woman you usually go out with, not experienced enough to travel in your league. You do have to admit that you have a rather casual attitude toward the women you date. I don't believe Angie can handle that type of a…well…that type of a no-strings-attached casual situation."

Ty fought to keep the anger out of his voice. "Open your eyes and look around. Angie is not that little girl you lived with before you went away to college. She's an intelligent, mature woman capable of making her own decisions. If she wants your advice, I'm sure she'll ask you for it."

Mac's expression turned very serious, his intense gaze almost becoming an adversarial glare. "I don't want her to be an innocent pawn in one of your *it's only fun and games* interludes. I don't want to see her get hurt.''

Ty returned Mac's pointed attitude with one of his own. ''Are you telling me I'm not good enough to go out with your sister? Are you telling me I have to stop seeing her and if I don't there will be consequences for me to deal with? I want to know exactly what you're trying to say so that there won't be any mistake or misunderstanding between us.''

''I'm just saying that Angie is a young, inexperienced girl. Her emotions and feelings could be easily hurt, even if that wasn't your intention. I...uh...'' Mac glanced down, uneasiness and a hint of uncertainty covering his features. ''I don't know what has gone on between you and Angie, but I don't want to see her hurt because you've made her think you're offering her a relationship with a future when all you're really offering her is a one-night stand. She's already been hurt by one broken engagement.''

Mac's words caught Ty off guard. ''Broken engagement? I didn't know she'd been engaged.''

''Yes, she was engaged for a while to a man from Portland...Caufield Woodrow III.''

''What happened?''

''She told me the engagement was off, but I don't know what happened or why. I don't know which one of them broke it off. She didn't volunteer the information and I didn't ask her. I don't want her to be hurt again by something she thinks is real when it's nothing more than another of your flings.''

A whole new level of discomfort pushed at Ty. He wanted out of the conversation and definitely wanted out of Mac's office. There was too much whirling around in his head. He blurted out the first thing that came to his mind. ''To tell you the truth, Mac…I don't see where it's anyone's business what has happened between Angie and me and that includes you. You may be her brother, but she's definitely an adult and does not need to answer to you or get your permission for anything. If she wants to see me, it's her choice and her decision.''

It pained Ty to utter the harsh words, but he needed to put an abrupt end to the conversation before even harsher things were said. Mac's words continued to ring in his ears…*nothing more than another of your flings.* The words had hurt. He felt as if Mac had verbally attacked him, had told him he wasn't good enough to be seeing Angie.

Ty put a stop to any further conversation when he turned and walked out of the office. Mac had hit a vulnerable place deep inside him, a place that had tried to work its way into his consciousness before, but he had never let it in. Now it seemed as if he was going to have to deal with the uncomfortable reality. He would need to face his own deeply buried doubts and fears. And even worse, he would have to explore his own vulnerability.

Ty went to his office, closed the door and slumped dejectedly into his chair. He had been walking on cloud nine when he arrived at work. Now he felt himself sinking into the depths. Exactly what did he want out of life? Everything had been so perfect for the past several years. Even though he had a great deal of family money available to him, after college graduation he had gone to work for a company where his father had no holdings or even influence. He had been determined to make it on his own. He didn't want to owe anything to his parents. He did not want to depend on them or what they could provide.

During the five years following college, even though they were working for different companies, Mac and Ty had continued to pursue their dream of one day being business partners and having their own company. Then that day had finally arrived. Both men had worked very hard and they had made the company a phenomenal success. He had become wealthy within his own right, as had Mac. The future had truly seemed unlimited.

Now he was filled with doubts. Exactly what did the future hold for him on a personal level?

He wondered where he would be ten years from now. Would he be a forty-five-year-old playboy running after beach-bunny-type women half his age and organizing sailing parties? Would his life be without any personal goals? Without any purpose other than his work? Would his future be devoid of that one special person to share both his successes and failures with? It was not a very appealing picture, one that left him as frightened as did his feelings for Angie.

His brow furrowed into a scowl. What about Angie's ex-fiancé—some guy named Caufield Woodrow III? Even the name grated against his nerves. It sounded so pretentious and pompous.

And it left him with a sinking feeling of trepidation.

And what about Angie? Exactly what did she want for the future? So many times she had brought up company business and their possible expansion plans. He had treated it as no more than casual conversation. Had she been trying to ask for his help in some way and he had been too dense to realize it? Too blinded by his own desires to worry about her ambitions and inner concerns—about what she wanted out of life? But if she wanted his help with something, why didn't she just come out and ask him?

The soul-searching moment left him very uncomfortable and uncertain.

He raked his gaze slowly around his office, taking in the details of his accomplishments. He was proud of the many awards the company had received for both excellence in the workplace and also for their many charitable contributions and civic activities. He and Mac had been so completely in agreement on every facet of the company's growth. They had always seemed to be a perfect example of a well-honed working relationship.

Yet they were so different in many ways. He loved parties and Mac preferred to stay at home. He had the ability to mingle at both social and business functions, to engage in casual chitchat with anyone, while Mac had admitted on more than one occasion that he was very uncomfortable in large groups, especially with strangers, and was not any good at maintaining a relationship—which explained Mac's broken engagement of a few years ago.

As a self-admitted workaholic, Mac had often said that he preferred to stay hidden away doing his designs and allow Ty to deal with clients, public relations, company personnel and other people-oriented business functions. Ty had long maintained that Mac needed someone to bring him out of his workaholic world and into the realm of real life.

A bittersweet chuckle escaped Ty's throat. How strange it was to have everything change in the space of just a few minutes. He and Mac were at odds with each other for the first time in their lives and it felt terrible. And what about his feelings for Angie? He had no idea what to do about that. An involuntary frown crossed his forehead. Mac was not the only one who had difficulty with relationships.

He looked around his office again as he pulled in a deep breath, then slowly exhaled. Oxygen had seemingly become scarce. The four walls suddenly felt as if they were closing in on him. He needed to get away, even if it was only for a few hours. He had to lighten the oppressive weight that had settled on his shoulders. He rose from his chair and walked to the window.

Something that never failed to clear his head when he had problems was sailing—the brisk ocean breeze, the smell of the salt air, the sensation of skimming effortlessly across the water. It was the most totally freeing activity he knew. He checked his schedule for the day—one appointment late that afternoon and it wasn't crucial.

He walked out of his office and down the hall toward the lobby. He couldn't stop himself from glancing into Mac's office as he passed the door. Mac was staring at him, his expression part anger and part bewilderment. He kept walking.

He stopped at the receptionist's desk. "Ellen, I'll be gone for the rest of the day. Could you call Stu McMahon and reschedule our appointment? Perhaps sometime tomorrow afternoon if that's convenient for him."

"Sure thing, Ty. Is there some place where you can be reached in case of an emergency?"

He paused for a moment as he turned her question over in his mind. He would have his cell phone with him, but...

"No—I can't be reached until this evening."

"But what if Mac needs you for something?"

He glanced toward the hallway and saw Mac approaching. He turned his attention back to Ellen. "I'm sure he won't be needing me for anything."

Ellen shot him a quizzical look which he chose to ignore. With that, Ty left the building, got in his car and drove away without looking back.

He headed for his house, but when he reached the turnoff to go to Mac's house it was as if his car had a mind of its own. Sailing was his passion and so was Angie. The only thing better than sailing would be to have Angie with him on his sailboat. He turned the corner and drove toward Mac's house.

Somehow he had to block out the harsh words he had exchanged with Mac and put their disagreement behind him. He knew it would not be easy. Mac's words and the implication of what he was saying had hurt him. And even more than that, they had hit his deepest buried spot of vulnerability and insecurity.

A moment later Angie answered the door in response to his knock. She was dressed in her robe and didn't look as if she'd been up very long. What she did look like was the most enchanting woman he had ever known and one he knew he couldn't stop seeing no matter what it might cost him.

"Ty...this is a surprise." She stepped aside to let him in. "What are you doing here so early? It's barely nine o'clock. Shouldn't you be at work?"

He flashed a warm smile as a soft glow of contentment spread through his body easing the memory of his clash with Mac. "You sound like you're not happy to see me." He pulled her into his arms and held her. It all felt so right.

"Of course I'm glad to see you. I'm just surprised, that's all."

"I've decided to take the day off and go sailing." He drew back just far enough to place his fingers beneath her chin and lift until he could look into her eyes. He brushed a sensual but brief kiss across her lips. "And I would be honored if you would go with me."

"Taking the day off work? You didn't say anything about that last night. Was this a sudden decision?"

"Yes, very sudden. I need to get away and clear my head. Do you know how to sail?"

"I've been sailing a few times, but only as a passenger. I've never been part of the crew, but I'd love to learn."

His grin told how pleased he was with her answer. "I'll wait right here while you get dressed."

"I'll only be a few minutes."

He watched as she disappeared down the hallway toward the guest bedroom. He wandered around Mac's living room as he waited for her, his mind dashing from one topic to another almost faster than he could keep up with it. A moment later his cell phone rang. He checked the caller ID—the call came from Mac's private line in his office. He debated whether to answer it, then turned off the phone. He didn't want a confrontation with Mac, especially not with Angie in the next room. And he didn't want to say anything he would regret later. All he wanted was to get out on the water with Angie and let the ocean breeze carry away all his troubles, doubts and fears.

"I'm ready." Angie appeared in the living room. "Did I hear a phone ring?"

"It was just my cell phone, nothing important. I've turned it off so we won't be interrupted with any business matters. It will be a fun-filled day without any intrusions.''

He glanced at his watch. He wanted to get away from Mac's house as quickly as possible, before Mac decided to get in his car and head for home to check on Angie's whereabouts. The realization that he was purposely ducking his business partner sent a wave of sadness through him, a feeling he didn't like. His relationship with Mac had always been open, honest and aboveboard.

Another thought forced itself to the forefront. It was not a new thought. It was one that had run through his mind several times since he had walked out of Mac's office. Should he tell Angie what had happened? Tell her about his disagreement with Mac and what it was about? It was yet another question for which there was no simple answer, another question left floating around in his mind. He tried to push it aside. He wanted the day to be a carefree time spent with Angie, not a day filled with dark clouds and anxiety.

They drove to Ty's house. ''I'll change into my sailing clothes, then we'll head out.''

''Is there anything I can gather together to take to your sailboat? Food or drinks…anything like that?''

''Nope…'' He waved his hand toward the large window with the view of his private dock where two sailboats were moored, a large gleaming blue-and-white ketch and a small fourteen-foot white racing sloop. ''We'll be going out on the large one. It's hooked up to dockside power and I keep it stocked at all times, ready to go. The only thing missing is us.'' He brushed another kiss on her lips, paused a moment as he plumbed the depths of her eyes, then headed for his bedroom.

Ten minutes later they walked hand in hand toward the dock. As they approached the sloop Ty tugged on her hand to bring her to a halt. "Are you serious about wanting to learn how to sail?"

"Yes, very much so." She cocked her head as she studied him for a moment. "Would you teach me?"

"I've love to share my sailing expertise with you. Hasn't Mac ever taught you any sailing techniques? He goes sailing almost as often as I do. That's about the only thing that gets him out of the offices, that and his early-morning jogs."

He gestured toward the sloop. "This is the one where you really get to sail, where all of the work functions are done by hand rather than computer and machine. This is the one we'll use for your sailing lessons. Come on, I'll give you a quick tour."

He helped her on board. They spent about fifteen minutes looking around with Ty pointing out the sailing features. "I can easily handle her by myself, but for the more inexperienced sailor it's recommended that a crew of two be on board." A soft smile curled the corners of his mouth as he looked around the deck. "I've owned this one for almost twenty years, since I was a teenager. I worked, saved and bought it with my own money. I have a real sentimental attachment to it."

He then indicated the other side of the dock. "Today we'll be taking out the ketch." He shot a teasing grin in her direction. "For your first lesson…a sloop is single-masted with only one mainsail. My racing sloop has a trapeze and spinnaker sail in addition to the mainsail. A ketch has two masts."

He escorted her on board the larger sailboat, gave her a quick tour of the deck and the quarters below deck, then in another fifteen minutes they were under way. As soon as they left the dock Ty felt the burden lift from his shoulders and his spirit lighten. He never felt more free than he did on the ocean, especially under full sail. And having Angie with him only increased that awareness.

"What do you want me to do? As I said, I've never been part of the crew, but I'm a quick learner."

"We need to get out of here first and into open water. Then we can cut the engine and switch over to sail and wind power. This boat is equipped with the latest in sailing technology so that I can handle by myself what would normally take a crew of at least four to do. For the pure experience of hands-on sailing, though, I definitely prefer the small racing sloop."

His large, technologically equipped sailboat allowed him to entertain a beautiful woman on sailing jaunts with just the two of them on board without his time being taken with doing the work of sailing. It also allowed him to have several people on board for a party without needing a full crew.

The ketch also served as a test lab to check out the latest equipment and technological innovations before the company incorporated them into a design project. But it was the smaller sailboat that he enjoyed the most—the one that provided him with the greatest sense of freedom and escape.

And now he had someone very special to enjoy it with, someone who had even expressed an interest in learning about his favorite activity. Someone to share it with. None of the other women he dated had ever expressed any interest in learning how to do the work involved with sailing. They had only been interested in the party atmosphere. And for him that had been enough. But not anymore.

He glanced over at Angie, her eyes closed and her face tilted up toward the morning sun. His heart swelled in his chest and the feeling of total contentment settled over him. His workday may have started out on a disagreeable note, but the rest of the day would be perfect. It seemed that things were always perfect whenever he was with Angie.

The words he and Mac had exchanged swirled through his mind. A moment of darkness invaded his sunshine.

How could he continue his relationship with Angie without jeopardizing his friendship with Mac? Exactly what was his relationship with Angie? How could he convince Mac that he would never do anything to hurt Angie? It was a perplexing problem and he didn't see an immediate solution on the horizon.

Six

Angie watched as Ty expertly maneuvered the large boat from his private dock on Bainbridge Island out toward the open water of Puget Sound. Even though the weather was cool, especially on the water, he had dressed in cutoff jeans, deck shoes and a sweatshirt. He looked so at home, as if he was born to handle a sailboat. The contentment on his face clearly showed how much he loved it.

The afterglow of their lovemaking from the previous night continued to course through her veins. Everything about him was totally desirable and excited her more than she ever thought possible. She had lain awake for what seemed like hours after Ty had brought her back to Mac's house. She didn't want to leave his bed any more than he wanted her to, but they each knew it would be a disastrous decision for her to stay the night. She knew Mac would never understand the situation or accept her adult status that easily and especially in that manner.

She also knew she had to somehow shake her inner turmoil where her big brother was concerned. It wasn't that he intimidated her. Not really. It was just that she was so in awe of Mac she sometimes had difficulty expressing her true feelings around him, especially if those feelings were in opposition to his beliefs. How did she ever expect to convince him she was able to handle a career position with his company if she couldn't stand up to his erroneous assumptions about what she wanted and what was best for her?

And Ty...what did the future hold for the two of them? A shadow momentarily clouded her thoughts. Or did they even have a future together beyond what they were sharing now? There were so many unanswered questions in a life that had suddenly been beset by an overabundance of confusion and conflict that hadn't been there as recently as a week ago.

But for right now those questions would have to wait until some other time. It was a beautiful, sunny day. She was sailing with a man who meant more to her than she thought possible especially in such a short amount of time, more than any other man ever had. Was she truly in love? She still wasn't sure, but after their night of unbridled passion she knew the answer was very close at hand. What would that do to her goals and career plans for the future? She wasn't sure of anything anymore.

The sailboat moved along gracefully through the water. Ty and Angie bonded together in an emotional encounter that equaled and perhaps passed their physical relationship. Ty explained some of the basics of sailing to her—setting the sails, running lines, securing the boom arm, tacking. He demonstrated some of the new technological equipment that had been installed such as GPS, mechanical raising and lowering of the sails so that it didn't need to be done by hand, computer navigation system and an automatic pilot system. He also pointed out standard equipment such as depth sounder, radar reflector, wind speed and direction indicator and satellite phone.

He loved the hands-on aspects of sailing. He always felt so alive and contented when he was out on the ocean. It was the same excitement he had experienced the very first time he went sailing as a child, an enthusiasm that had increased over the years rather than diminishing.

He glanced toward Angie. A sensation of warmth and caring settled over him. And now he had found the same type of excitement and contentment with her.

Ty reached out and took her hand. "Are you hungry? It's a little past lunchtime."

"Yes, I could use something to eat."

He dropped anchor in a sheltered cove off one of the many small uninhabited islands in the San Juan Islands group. He went to the galley below and brought lunch up on deck. He spread it out like a picnic. They ate while enjoying the beautiful scenery and engaging in casual conversation. When they finished, he cleared away their picnic remains.

"Oh, Ty, this is marvelous." Her face beamed with pleasure. "I can certainly see why you love sailing so much. What a sense of freedom and exhilaration." Her gaze locked with his. Her voice grew softer. "Thank you for sharing it with me."

He pulled her into his arms and placed a loving kiss on her lips. "I'm glad you're enjoying it. If you'd like,

I'll take you out on my other sailboat as soon as possible so you can get some hands-on experience with sailing."

"I'd like that very much."

He reveled in the closeness, the sense of oneness he felt with her. "Maybe we could take a trip...sail down to Mexico, maybe Cabo San Lucas...just the two of us." There had been more emotion in his voice than he intended, more than he wanted to show. The feelings coursing through him were so foreign to anything he had ever felt before that he didn't know how to handle them.

"That sounds wonderful." Angie snuggled into his embrace. *Wonderful* hardly described the scene that flashed through her mind. Warm breezes, bright sunlight on sandy beaches, brilliant blue skies and Ty's arms wrapped around her. Long nights of passionate lovemaking under the silvery glow of the moon. The delicious fantasy continued to play on the screen of her mind.

Then his mouth was on hers and all thoughts stopped. She circled her arms around his neck and allowed the sexy magnetism of Ty to pulse through her body. Her desires burst into flame as he slowly worked his hands inside the back of her jeans and panties until he cupped the roundness of her bare bottom. He pulled her body to him until he had her hips nestled against his.

His lips nibbled at the corners of her mouth and tugged at her earlobe. His words tickled across her cheek. "Have you ever made love on a sailboat?"

Her reply was as breathless as his question. "No...never."

"Would you like to?"

"Very much so." She knew no one would ever be able to excite her the way he did, to fulfill her every desire. Even though she hadn't known him that long, at least not as an adult, she was now sure that she had been falling in love with him from that first day when they had lunch together.

She wished she had some clue about his feelings toward her. She knew he liked her, liked touching her, liked being with her. But did he love her? She didn't know. And a commitment? She was reluctant to even bring up the subject. If he couldn't willingly offer her one, then to push him into something he didn't want was a sure way of losing him for good.

If this was all their relationship was ever going to be she wanted as much of it as possible. She reached inside his sweatshirt and ran her hands over the hard planes of his well-defined chest. She wanted everything. She wanted it all. Was that asking for too much?

His kiss deepened, infusing her with the heated passion she had come to associate with him. His tongue twined with hers as she welcomed each intimate caress. Her breathing grew ragged. It seemed as if all the oxygen had been sucked from the air. Tremors of delight rippled through her body, driving her desires to a higher plane.

His husky voice whispered in her ear. "Let's go down to the master stateroom." He took her hand and led her to the cabin. She watched as he pulled off his sweatshirt and kicked off his deck shoes. She reached for the snap on his cutoff jeans. He quickly pulled them off along with his briefs. There was an intense moment of eye contact, his smoldering gaze sending a wave of urgency sweeping through her.

Making love in the middle of the day—she had

never done anything that daring before. And on top of that, they were on a sailboat. It made her feel wildly uninhibited, earthy and almost decadent. Sex with her ex-fiancé had always been as structured and controlled as everything else about him. She loved the spontaneity and excitement that surrounded Ty. She loved the way it made her feel.

And she loved Ty.

He slowly pulled her shirt over her head and tossed it to the floor. The delight danced through his eyes as he cupped her bare breasts in his hands. His touch elicited a soft moan from her. She wanted her bare skin next to his, their bodies twined together. She kicked off her shoes, then unfastened her jeans, shoved them down her hips and stepped out of them.

He pulled her into his embrace, then lowered her to the bed. His mouth was on hers again, tempting her with the type of pleasure she knew would soon be coursing through her body in a heated flow of ecstasy. His hardened arousal pressed against her thigh, his fingers teasing her nipples into tautly puckered peaks.

She caressed his shoulders, then ran her hands across his muscled back. His mouth left a fiery trail of kisses across her cheek, down the side of her neck, at the base of her throat and finally at the valley nestled between her breasts. Every place he touched her produced a ripple of excitement. She gasped for air, her ragged breathing matching his. Only her bikini panties prevented the heat of his manhood from penetrating her moist core.

She jerked her head back into the pillow when his mouth closed over her nipple. She arched her back, pressing her body against his. The feel of his bare skin, his tightly drawn muscles, the heat of his passion…everything melted together leaving her wanting more and more. The gentle rocking of the boat added to the sensual cocoon that enveloped her.

He quickly shifted his attention to her other breast, teasing that nipple with the tip of his tongue before taking it into his mouth. A shiver of delight washed through her body. Layers of excitement built in intensity. She needed to touch him, to feel his hardened arousal. She reached for his manhood, stroking the rigid length until he shifted away from her grasp.

"Not yet—" His words came out as a barely discernable raspy whisper. "No need to rush things. I want to give you pleasure…again and again."

He ran his tongue along the underside of each breast, then trailed it down her stomach until he reached the elastic of her bikini panties. He tugged at them with his teeth, slowly inching them down her hips until he had exposed her most private recess. His breath tickled across the sensitive skin of her inner thighs, sending a convulsive wave coursing through her body. She wanted to touch him. She had to touch him. She reached down and ran her fingers across his shoulders, reveling in the sensation of his bare skin.

He slowly placed a series of kisses, each moving closer and closer to the heated core of her womanhood. Her senses teetered on the brink. Then he placed the most intimate kiss of all. She felt the gasp leave her throat as much as she heard it, followed by the exquisite rapture that exploded inside her.

Ty felt the shudder rush through her body accompanied by a throaty moan of delight. He pulled her panties down her legs and tossed them on top of his clothes on the floor. He reached his hands up to her breasts as she thrust herself more fully against his mouth. He had never known anyone so honestly responsive and delightfully sensual. Everything about her excited him more than any woman he had ever known. And it was far more than sexual fun and games. The entire package of personality, brains, compassion and beauty went with that sensuality to create the most complete woman he could ever hope to know and spend time with.

And plan a future with? It was a thought that invaded his mind more and more with each passing hour.

He reached for the drawer in the headboard of the bed and withdrew the condom packet. He rolled over on his back and a minute later he grasped her hips in his hands. He straddled her body across his with her knees on each side of his hips, then lifted and settled her onto his erection. Her femininity snuggly encased his hardness, sending a rush of heated intensity crashing through him. She was everything he had ever wanted, everything he had hoped for—and so much more.

They moved together in perfect unison, their lovemaking again propelling each of them to the heights of ecstasy. Their tempo increased as each neared the ultimate climax. Angie fell forward, her upper torso pressed against his body. Ty quickly rolled her over onto her back while maintaining the physical connection binding them together. He wanted the final release, yet he wanted the euphoria of their coupling to last forever.

His mouth claimed hers—devouring, demanding and giving as much as he took. His driving passions produced deeper and quicker strokes, each one met and equaled by the upward thrust of her hips.

She tightened her arms and legs around him as wave

after wave of exquisite ecstasy convulsed through her body.

A moment later the hard spasms shuddered through him. He held her close as he forced his breathing to a normal pattern. He continued to hold her body tightly against his. He didn't want to ever let go. He stroked his fingers through the silky tresses of her hair, then cradled her head against his shoulder. He didn't want to take a chance on losing her. It was a sobering thought that filled him with the type of contentment he had never before known...a contentment that left him as fearful of the implications as it did fulfilled.

Ty and Angie returned from their sailing day shortly after dark. They secured the boat at his private dock.

"I have a fairly busy schedule at work for the rest of this week, but the first day I can clear my calendar we'll take out the sloop and I'll give you your first sailing lesson. It will be work and you'll probably end up using muscles you didn't even know you had. So..." he shot her a teasing grin "...be prepared to be sore the next day. It's not everyone's idea of *fun*."

"I enjoy being on the water and if today is any example, I know I'm going to love it."

He pulled her into his arms. His voice took on a softness that spoke of the emotion coursing through him. "And I'm going to love teaching you, too."

"I read a couple of books about sailing so that I could at least be familiar with the terminology and have a better understanding of what the company does...you know, how things work and why something needs to be there. That sort of thing. I wanted to be conversant on the subject. I was going to ask Mac to teach me when he had some free time, but judging from what

I've seen so far I could be a little old lady before that time arrives.''

His easy laugh filled the air. ''You are so right.''

He brushed a kiss across her lips, then took her hand as they walked toward his house. It had been an ideal day filled with a perfect combination of carefree fun and heated passion. She was everything he wanted, everything he could hope for.

So why were his insides knotted into a hard lump and his nerves dancing on edge? If only he had some insight into what she expected from him. Or, more accurately, what she assumed the future held.

He tried to convince himself that things were very good just the way they were. They had an unspoken bond between them. There was no need to talk about commitment to a relationship—no need to make those promises that other people seemed to believe were necessary. That's what he wanted to believe, but the thought left him as unsettled as he had been before. He didn't want to lose her, but it seemed to him that they had managed to establish a relationship without having discussed it. There was no reason to talk about commitment now, to verbalize what was already happening.

He knew from experience that making promises and even signing the paperwork to make it legal didn't guarantee that a relationship would work out, that it would be lasting. It wasn't the words or the piece of paper that made a relationship. It was how two people felt and how they behaved toward each other.

He stopped walking for a moment, then pulled her into his embrace. He continued to hold her. In spite of his attempt to dismiss his concerns, the question continued to circulate through his mind. What had been a remote concern began to loom larger and larger in his reality.

What exactly were his feelings toward her, his concept for the future? Just how involved had he become? He tried to force the fragmented thoughts and feelings to crystallize into a single thought that would clarify things, but each time he came near the word *love,* the one word that would define everything, he panicked and shoved it away. All he knew for certain was that it truly frightened him.

He gathered his determination and reinforced his long-held belief. Commitment was nothing but a word and didn't have anything to do with how two people felt about each other. His inner turmoil began to subside. Things between them were great, so why mess it up with a bunch of unnecessary conversation and useless words about commitment and relationships?

He forced a false sense of confidence. Things were perfect just as they were. The two of them were already sharing their time, their passion and their emotions. That was everything. That was all they needed. They continued on to the house, walking hand in hand.

Once inside, he built a fire in the fireplace and opened a bottle of wine. They sat in front of the fire and watched the flames dance across the logs. Warmth surrounded them, enfolding them in a soft cloak of delight, caring and contentment.

As perfect as the day had been, Angie found herself wrestling with the underlying uncertainties of what path she needed to follow. Her once single-minded objective to procure a career position with Mac's company had been wrenched sharply off-track by her unexpected involvement—she didn't know what else to call it, she didn't feel comfortable using the word *re-*

lationship—with Ty. If only she knew where things stood between them.

It was a theme that continued to play over and over in her mind, something she realized she was beginning to obsess about. Each time she started to dwell on it, she tried to shove it away. It seemed to occupy more and more of her thoughts and had become a towering obstacle for her.

Could she count on his help in approaching Mac with her desired goal? Would he be a part of her future or would working in the same environment end up being awkward for each of them? It had all been so clear in her mind the day she arrived at Mac's house from Portland. Then she was swept into a whirling vortex of passion and emotion by the name of Tyler Farrell. Now nothing was clear. If only she could ease her mind and stop dwelling on it.

A moment later a tingle of excitement rippled through her as Ty's lips brushed across her nape, nibbled at her earlobe, then captured her mouth with an intense kiss that left her reeling and her concerns scattered to the far corners of the wind. Yes…she loved him. She loved this playboy who lived in the fast lane and seemed to already have everything he wanted.

And what she wanted more than anything was him.

Their lovemaking on the sailboat had been even more spine-tingling and all-consuming than the previous night in Ty's bedroom. It was as if they couldn't get enough of each other. Only the late-afternoon hour and the need to return home brought a temporary calm to the desires that continued to sizzle just below the surface—to the sensual heat she suspected would never be completely cooled.

He ran his hand beneath her shirt and up her rib

cage, his fingers tickling along her skin until he reached her bare breast. The moment he brushed his fingertips against her nipple her desires exploded into a world of need and want just as they had that afternoon. He teased her nipples with his tongue until they formed taut peaks.

She had never felt so free, uninhibited or sexy as she did when she was with him. She reached for the snap on his cutoff jeans. She didn't hesitate as she unfastened them. She marveled at her own aggressiveness and blatant audacity as she lowered his zipper. She bent forward and kissed his growing hardness through the fabric as it pressed against the front of his briefs.

The doorbell rudely interrupted the rapidly escalating need that enfolded them in a cocoon of heated desires and rekindled passions. The same disappointment that swept through her body was mirrored in his eyes. His husky words told of his level of arousal. ''Do you suppose whoever it is will go away if we ignore the doorbell?''

The incessant ringing continued. She emitted a soft sigh of resignation. ''Apparently not.''

Ty reluctantly turned loose of her. They each adjusted their clothes and made a valiant attempt at regaining their composure. He placed a tender kiss on her lips, then turned his attention toward the front door. His annoyance came out in his voice and surrounded every word as he spoke. ''Someone is much too persistent for their own good and I believe that's exactly what I'm going to tell them.''

A combination of surprise and anxiety shot through Ty when he yanked open the door and found Mac standing on his porch—certainly the last person he expected or wanted to see at that moment. He maintained his stance, neither stepping aside nor asking Mac to come in. He forced a calm to his voice, but couldn't keep the coolness out of it. "Is there something I can do for you?"

Mac nervously shifted his weight from one foot to the other. "May I come in?"

Ty paused for a moment as he decided what to do. His first inclination was to protect Angie from embarrassment. He finally stepped aside and motioned for Mac to come in. "Sure."

Ty remained in the foyer, not volunteering to move any farther into the house. "So, what brings you here? Did I miss a meeting? Forget to do a report?" He made no attempt to keep the sarcasm and irritation out of his voice. "I didn't check with you before I left the offices? What?"

"I've been trying to reach you all day, both on your cell phone and here at your house."

"It was a beautiful day so I decided to go sailing. I had my cell phone turned off because I didn't want to be bothered."

"I…uh…I thought we might talk."

Ty leveled a steady look at Mac. He wasn't sure where this was going, but he did know it made him uncomfortable. "Okay…what do you want to talk about?"

Mac's exasperation covered his features. "You're not going to make this easy, are you?"

"Make what easy? You haven't told me why you're here and I certainly wouldn't want to make any assumptions about what might be on your mind."

Ty inwardly winced at the harshness of the words he had just spoken. He and Mac had never been at odds before and he didn't like the feeling, but he still hurt from Mac's attitude that morning—from the thinly veiled assertions that he wasn't good enough for Angie. The brief confrontation with Mac had done more than upset him. It had also opened the door on his concerns and fears about his own future on a personal level, something that left him decidedly confused and troubled about what to do.

Mac's words became louder and took on a level of irritation. "Look, Ty, I don't know what you imagined that I said—"

"Imagined?" Ty's volume increased to match that of his business partner. The anger he had been trying to control refused to stay tucked away. "I heard you very clearly. There was no doubt you were telling me to stay away from Angie—that I wasn't good enough to go out with your sister."

"That's not what I meant. I was merely trying to point out that she's too young and inexperienced to handle your lifestyle. I don't think you should—"

"Stop it!" Angie's shouted command broke into the rapidly escalating disagreement between the two men. They turned toward the sound. She stood framed in the doorway leading to the den. She looked from one man to the other as she walked toward them.

Ty moved quickly to intercept her. His voice softened as it filled with emotion. "Angie—"

Mac started to speak. "I came here straight from the office, Angie. I didn't know you were—"

"The two of you…just stop it!" A combination of anger and emotional upheaval filled her voice, but she didn't care. "I can't stand seeing this happen." She glared at both men. She felt as if her entire life was being torn apart. On one side was the brother she idolized and on the other side was the man she loved. She had never experienced such a helpless feeling as the sinking realization about what was happening settled over her.

"You two have never argued about anything and here you are suddenly yelling at each other." Her voice cracked as she fought to keep a sob from escaping her throat. "I don't know what started it or why, but I do know that I'm to blame."

Mac immediately tried to smooth over the situation. "Don't be silly, Angie. It's just a little misunderstanding—"

She made no attempt to curb her growing anger. "Don't do that to me again. Stop patronizing me, Mac. Stop telling me not to be silly as if I had no concept of what was going on around me. I'm a grown woman, but you're always treating me like a child. I'm twenty-four years old. Think back to the time you were twenty-four. Did you need to be protected from everything and everyone? Were you incapable of making intelligent and mature decisions? Did you need someone to constantly pat you on the head in a condescending manner while telling you to stop being silly and not worry your cute little head about things?"

A look of shock spread across Mac's face. "I don't do that."

"The hell you don't!" All of Angie's pent-up frustration with the situation finally overruled her feelings of intimidation and awe where her brother was concerned. For the first time she gave free rein to her anger. "I wanted only one thing when I arrived here. I wanted to work for your company."

Mac was at an obvious loss about how to respond to this very uncharacteristic outburst. "But all you had to do was—"

''I don't want an entry-level position like the one you mentioned in the note you left me on the refrigerator door—I'm not interested in a receptionist position that has nothing to do with my education or my work experience. I don't want the type of job you'd hand to me just because I asked, something that would be yet another instance of you taking care of me. I want a career position where I can prove to you that I'm good at what I do. Something where I can make a viable contribution to the company. You've never noticed anything about me beyond that little girl.''

She paused a moment to take a calming breath, but not long enough for Mac to get in a word. Now that she had started, she didn't want to stop until she said everything that was on her mind. ''Don't get me wrong, I truly and deeply appreciate everything you've done for me. I know there's no way I'll ever be able to repay you.''

Then she blurted out the words before she could stop them. ''But more than anything I want your respect for me as an adult, to be treated as an equal.''

The tears welled in her eyes, but she quickly blinked them away before they trickled down her cheeks. She glanced at Ty, then returned her attention to her brother. All the steam had suddenly gone out of her. Her voice dropped to a near whisper. ''But it seems that the only thing I've accomplished is to cause a rift between the two of you.''

This time she could not blink away the tears. She turned away, hoping to prevent anyone from seeing them slowly overflow the brims of her eyes and make their way down her cheeks. She had not meant to explode like that, but now it was too late to stop it or take back anything she had said. At that moment more than anything she wanted the warmth and comfort of Ty's arms around her, to be enfolded in his embrace where she could feel safe and secure. She stole a quick glance toward Ty. He seemed totally bewildered.

A horrible rush of embarrassment engulfed her. She had just made a fool of herself in front of the two men who were the most important people in her life. She had to get away. She needed time to think, to collect herself. She grabbed her purse and dashed toward the door.

Ty attempted to grab her arm, but she pulled away. He called to her. "Angie, wait—" The door slammed and she was gone before he could stop her. The two men stared at each other in stunned silence. The expression of shock and confusion on Mac's face mirrored the upheaval churning inside Ty.

It was Ty who made the first move toward the door with Mac closely behind him. He raced outside and came to a halt in the middle of the driveway. He looked up and down the street, but didn't see any sign of her. It was as if the night had literally swallowed her up. He fought the increasing level of panic that tried to take over.

He turned toward Mac. The intense emotions running through him came out in his voice. "Where could she have gone? Does she know anyone else here?"

Mac seemed as perplexed as Ty. "I don't know. Maybe she's walking back to my house."

Ty stood riveted to the spot, staring at Mac without really seeing him. His mind seemed to be going in several directions at once, but two conflicting thoughts tried to crowd out all the others—was Angie all right and what had she meant by her statement of single-minded determination in procuring a job with Mac?

An uneasy feeling began to rise inside him. Could their being together possibly be nothing more than a ruse to get him to help her? Was she such a good actress that she had been able to totally deceive him? Convince him that she cared about him rather than what he might be able to do for her? No—he refused to accept that idea. It was a thought he didn't like, one that he desperately wanted to be able to dismiss. A myriad of emotions became so tightly entwined that he didn't know what he was feeling from one minute to the next.

He tried to pull some logic into the situation. The first thing he had to do was make sure Angie was all right. Then he needed to figure out what was happening, what was real and what was nothing more than his desires overruling the pragmatic side of his nature. Exactly what were her feelings about him...about them as a couple in a relationship?

There—he had finally put the concept of a relationship into a concrete thought, but it didn't make anything any clearer than it had been a moment earlier. It only made him more fearful of what the future held.

"—home to see if she's there. I'll check the route along the way to see if I can find her."

Mac's words jerked Ty back to the present. "Uh...yes. And I'll go the other direction and see if I can find her walking along the street. But first I'll check the dock and my sailboat. She might have gone there."

His mind immediately drifted to the day they had spent together on his sailboat—a day filled with both heated passion and the quiet contentment of just being together. It had been the most perfect day he had ever spent with anyone and something he didn't want to lose. He knew in his heart that she was incapable of dishonesty, that she had not been misrepresenting herself or attempting to manipulate him to her predetermined agenda.

Only now everything had turned upside down. He and Mac had been at odds for the first time in their lives. Angie had stormed out of his house angry and hurt and he wasn't sure exactly why.

He collected his thoughts and composure. ''You've got your cell phone? Let me know if you find her and I'll do the same.''

Ty watched as Mac climbed in his car, backed out of the driveway and started slowly down the street. Ty walked around the side of his house toward the back deck. He then proceeded across the yard to the dock.

He checked the large ketch first, searching the deck then methodically going through each of the areas below deck. When that proved fruitless, he searched the smaller sloop but to no avail.

He had been so sure he would find her on one of the sailboats. Now uncertainty and fear filled him with dread. He tried to analyze her words about the job and it being her only reason for being there. Exactly what type of impact would that have on the future...on their future together?

Ty returned to the house to get his car keys so he could search for her along the road. He had just crossed the deck and reached for the doorknob of the back door when his cell phone rang.

He quickly checked the caller ID before answering it. ''Mac?''

''I just got home. She's not here and I didn't see her anywhere along the way.''

''I've checked the grounds and both sailboats. She's not here, either. I'm putting my home phone on call forwarding so everything will go to my cell phone. You wait there in case she shows up and I'll make a circle through the village, then continue on to your house.''

He glanced at his watch. It was only eight-thirty, but it felt so much later. He tried to put an objective spin on things. She was an adult, not a child. It wasn't the middle of the night and it was a very safe neighborhood. What disturbed him the most was how upset and angry she had been when she slammed out of his house. Another ripple of anxiety shot through him, then settled in the pit of his stomach where it continued to churn as he climbed into his car.

Seven

Ty drove into the village. He parked and went into several stores, a couple of restaurants and even a bar looking for her, but she wasn't there. She wasn't anywhere. He continued on to Mac's house. He found Mac standing on the front porch, cell phone in one hand and cordless phone from the house in the other hand. Mac started down the walkway toward the street, meeting Ty halfway.

"Well?" The apprehension in Mac's voice was unmistakable. "Did you find her?"

Ty shook his head in despair. "No." He slumped into one of the chairs on the front porch. It had been a long time since he'd felt so dejected and been so completely at a loss about what to do.

The strained atmosphere between the two men intensified as silence descended over them. Ty knew he should say something, but he didn't know what to say or how to broach the subject. He and Mac had never argued in their lives and this one was particularly painful because of the personal nature and the fact that it involved Angie.

"Well...I'm back."

Mac whirled around and Ty jumped up from the chair at the sound of Angie's voice.

A tinge of embarrassment spread across Angie's face. "Assuming I'm still welcome to stay here."

"Don't be ridiculous. Of course you're welcome." Mac quickly moved toward Angie. He put his arm around her shoulder in a protective manner. "Are you all right?"

"I'm fine." She glanced at the ground, her voice dropping off to a whisper. "I just needed a little time to cool off." She hesitated as she tried to find the right words, then looked up to meet her brother's gaze. "I'm sorry, Mac. I didn't mean to explode at you like that."

"I had no idea you felt that way..." A teasing grin played around the corners of his mouth. "Or that you had such a temper."

A sheepish look crossed Mac's face. "And I didn't realize I was treating you like that. I've always wanted what was best for you, Angie. You know that. I would never want to hold you back or make you feel like you needed to settle for less than what you could be or what you wanted out of life."

"I know."

Mac pulled her into a warm, brotherly hug. "Forgive me?"

She returned his warmth with a smile. "You know I do."

It had been an outburst of emotion, but Angie had finally managed to tell Mac what her original plan had

been. Only now she wasn't as sure exactly what she
wanted or what the future held. It was the uppermost
thought that occupied her mind as she walked from
Ty's house toward Mac's house, intentionally taking a
roundabout route. She wanted the time alone without
either Mac or Ty finding her as she walked down the
street. She needed to be able to think without either
one of them pulling at her emotions.

And what about Ty? She was aware of the new problem she had created with her outburst. Had he misin-
terpreted what she said? Did he think she had been
using him? Manipulating him for her own selfish purposes? Had she irreparably damaged her relationship
with him? She caught a glimpse of Ty, noting the combination of relief and confusion that covered his face.
She stole a brief moment of eye contact with him. A
whole new level of uneasiness welled inside her.

Ty looked away. He tried to put everything Angie
had said into some sort of cohesive picture. Her explosion had stunned him. She had arrived from Portland
with a predetermined plan. Had he been part of that
plan from the very beginning? Was what had been happening between them part of that plan as well? Her
angry outburst in the foyer of his house showed a
whole new side of her, one that harbored fire and determination. Even though the entire matter had him bewildered, he liked the sparks she generated. She was
definitely a woman who knew her own mind, someone
with substance rather than the clinging vine that so
many of the women he dated seemed to be.

He felt the frown lines wrinkle across his forehead
as he turned his gaze toward Mac. After all of this,
where did he and Mac stand? Would this strain on their

working and personal relationship end up being a permanent rift that would cause future problems?

Ty wasn't sure what to do or what to think. "Uh...well...since everything seems to be okay here, I guess I'd better be heading for home." He needed time to sort things out and determine exactly what it was that he wanted. He had two major problems to resolve—patching things up with Mac and setting his priorities about Angie. Maybe things would look better in the morning after a good night's sleep, but a sinking feeling told him it wasn't going to be that easy.

Angie's voice broke into his thoughts. "I'll walk you to your car."

She glanced at Mac. "I'll be right back." Mac hesitated as if he wanted to say something, then turned and went inside the house.

"Are you okay, Angie?" Ty reached out and grasped her hand. Her touch was warm and inviting and sent the same feeling of life fulfillment through him that he found so reassuring whenever he was with her.

A touch of irritation crept into her voice. "I wish everyone would stop asking me that."

She took a calming breath, then held his gaze for several seconds before speaking. "I think I owe you an apology. I had no right to lose my temper like that, especially in your home. It's just that I couldn't stand listening to you and Mac at each other like that, especially knowing it was my fault."

"You don't owe me an apology. And nothing was your fault." But he knew that he and Angie did need to talk. He wanted to know about her plan for a job and how—or if—he fit into that plan. He wanted to know where things stood between them, but he wasn't sure how to find out without delving into his anxieties and squarely confronting his fear of commitment and relationships head-on.

He squeezed her hand and gave her a confident smile. ''We can talk tomorrow. I'm sure things will look better in the morning.''

He still didn't believe the words even as he said them out loud. He simply hadn't known what else to say to smooth over the awkward situation. And the harsh words he and Mac had exchanged still loomed large in his mind. The one thing he did know was that he couldn't allow the problem to fester until it became insurmountable.

He stole a quick glance toward the house in an attempt to see if Mac was watching them. He leaned forward and placed a loving kiss on her lips, but not one that could be misconstrued by anyone looking on. ''I'll call you tomorrow.'' He climbed into his car and drove away.

Angie returned to the house where she found Mac nervously pacing up and down the living room. He looked up as she entered the room, offering her a tentative smile.

''Do you feel like talking? I'm all yours if you want to discuss this job thing.''

Angie sank into a large chair, curling her legs under her. She leveled a steady look at her brother. ''I think right now I'd rather discuss what you and Ty were arguing about. I heard him say you told him not to see me anymore. Is that what you told him?''

Mac nervously cleared his throat and attempted a teasing grin. ''Does this mean we're going to have our first adult conversation?''

"Don't you think it's about time? And you're patronizing me again. Stop it."

Mac drew in a deep breath, then slowly exhaled as he shook his head. "You hit me with a lot of stuff all at once, certainly not what I was expecting when you arrived a little over a week ago. I thought I'd finish my design project, help you get a job with one of our clients and assist you in getting moved into your own apartment."

He looked up at her. "Instead, you've been dating my business partner. You inform me I've been treating you like a child. Instead of finding a job in Seattle, you tell me that what you really wanted when you arrived here was a career position with our company." He studied her for a moment. "What I've found out is that the kid sister I thought I knew has turned out to be a woman I don't know at all."

He flashed an engaging and sincere smile. "Yes, I think it's probably about time for us to have an adult conversation."

Mac and Angie talked long into the night. She told him about her work experience in Portland, why she left the company and what she wanted to do with her life. She gave him her ideas on the type of position she thought she could most effectively handle in the company if they went ahead with their expansion plans and also where she thought she could fit in if they didn't. She made it clear that she had given it a lot of intelligent thought.

For his part, Mac filled her in on his thoughts for the expansion. He explained what the design project was that he had been working on and how it related to the expansion. They exchanged thoughts and suggestions on various facets of the company.

Everything about their discussion excited her. It was as if she had gotten a new lease on life and discovered a new side to her brother that she had never known. Suddenly he didn't seem to be that same larger-than-life person she had always been in awe of and who slightly intimidated her. He had become just her brother again, someone she still looked up to and respected but at the same time someone she could now talk to on an equal level—as an adult.

However, as favorably as the conversation had gone the one thing they did not discuss was her relationship with Ty. It was almost as if everything was going so well that neither one of them wanted to introduce a topic that could cause a whole new area of dissension and put a damper on what they had accomplished.

Mac glanced at his watch. "I don't believe it. Do you know it's almost two o'clock in the morning? We've been talking for hours."

Angie stifled a yawn as she rose from her chair. "I don't know about you, but I think they've been some of the most positive and productive hours I've spent in a long time."

Mac offered a slightly weary smile. "Is it okay if I still hug you from time to time or is that too childish?"

"I'd be disappointed if you didn't." She put her arms around his waist. "Thank you, Mac."

"For what?"

"For listening to me. For letting me air my frustrations."

"In the future, if you have a complaint with me don't let it go until it becomes a huge problem. Let me know." He smiled at her. "Even if you have to hit me over the head with a sledgehammer to get my attention."

Angie flashed a big grin. "You've got it."

They said good-night and she retired to the guest room. One problem still remained, one they had not discussed but she knew the day would come when they would have to—Tyler Farrell. She still didn't know specifically what Mac and Ty had been arguing about other than it had to do with her dating Ty and Mac disapproving.

Even though Mac had professed his acceptance of her as an adult, he had carefully steered the conversation away from Ty and she had let him do it. Other than to tell Mac that who she chose to date was her business and not his, she didn't know what to say to him. Until she knew exactly what type of a relationship she had with Ty, there was nothing for her and Mac to talk about. She couldn't tell her brother that she loved Ty when she didn't have a clue about Ty's real feelings toward her.

It was a topic she knew she should be discussing with Ty, not with Mac.

Thoughts and concerns continued to swirl around in her head leaving her as confused about where she and Ty were headed as she had been before. If only she could get a handle on what was in Ty's head...and in his heart.

Ty paced up and down his office floor, glancing at his watch and pausing to stare down the hallway each time he passed the door. His impatience grew with each passing minute. He had made a point of arriving at his office very early that morning in hopes of catching Mac before the other employees arrived.

He had endured a restless night, his mind filled with conflicting thoughts and confusion. It seemed that he had spent a great deal of his time lately wrestling with confusion. The only time he truly felt at peace was when he and Angie were together. Whenever they were apart his inner turmoil would once again take charge in an attempt to cripple his logic.

After what felt like an eternity he finally heard Mac unlock his office door. Ty took a calming breath, then a second one. He and Mac had to talk this out and now would be best, before either of them became involved in the day's work and while the events of last night were still fresh. He took a third deep breath, held it for several seconds, then slowly exhaled. He headed down the hall, the anxiety churning in the pit of his stomach.

Ty paused at Mac's office door. "Do you have a few minutes?"

Mac turned around at the sound of Ty's voice. A look of caution spread across his features. "Uh… sure."

Ty entered the office and closed the door behind him before settling into the large chair across from Mac's desk. He had been giving it a lot of thought and had decided that straight out was the only way to handle what could turn out to be a volatile situation. He also knew it had to be done now before things became even more strained to the point where it could start having an impact on the business.

Ty nervously cleared his throat. "We need to talk." He held up his hand to silence Mac when his partner started to say something. "And don't ask me what we need to talk about. You know as well as I do that we need to talk about your objections to me dating Angie."

"Yes…well, Angie and I talked until almost two this morning."

"Did you discuss your own problems or did I become part of that discussion?"

Mac glanced at the floor, his voice becoming less sure. "We...uh...didn't get around to you."

"Then perhaps you and I should *get around to me* now. You've made it very clear that you disapprove of me dating Angie, although you haven't given me a specific reason...just some generalities about different lifestyles. I feel compelled to repeat what I said the other day. Angie is a grown woman who is capable of making her own decisions. You may—"

"Please, stop right there." Mac held up his hand. "She's already made me aware of that reality—emphatically and more than once, I might add."

Ty cocked his head and shot a questioning look at his partner. "And?"

Mac glanced at the floor again, as if trying to compose the right words before speaking. "And after she went to bed I spent most of the rest of the night thinking about what she had said."

Mac looked up and caught a moment of eye contact with Ty. "She really got me with that comment she made at your house about thinking back to when I was twenty-four and whether I was able to make intelligent decisions on my own. I decided she was right. To the rest of the world she may have become an adult, but in my mind she had remained that little girl I needed to protect and take care of."

"To get everything out in the open and up-front, I want you to know that I have every intention of continuing to date Angie. I don't know where it's going, or if it's even going anywhere at all, but in the meantime we enjoy each other's company and have a good time. So, where does this leave you and me?"

A hint of concern darted across Mac's face. "For starters, I don't want to know what *having a good time* means. I'm willing to accept her adult status, but that doesn't mean I want to know everything." His expression turned serious. "Bottom line—it was wrong of me to keep her categorized in that neatly boxed-in place even though I wasn't aware I was doing it. The two of you dating is your business and not something for me to judge."

"I'm glad you and Angie worked things out, but I still don't know where it leaves us." Ty leveled a steady gaze at Mac, one that belied the trepidation pushing at his insides. "Does everything go back to the way it was with the past few days being just an unfortunate little incident that can be forgotten, or is this tension going to continue with us being outwardly polite while sticking solely to business?"

Mac took a deep breath. He sat in the other large chair on the same side of his desk as Ty. "You ask tough questions and put me in an uncomfortable position. Angie is my sister, my kid sister, regardless of how much of an adult she is now. She grew up without a father and being the oldest brother I partially assumed that position in her life. It's a difficult role to relinquish, especially after all these years."

Anxiety rose inside Ty. Mac was not the only one finding himself in an uncomfortable position. He knew he needed to give Mac some sort of reassurance about his intentions toward Angie, but exactly what were those intentions? He still didn't know beyond the fact that he wanted her to be part of his life.

Ty rose from his chair. "I can only say that I care about Angie very much and would never do anything to hurt her. Beyond that...well, I guess she and I will have to find out for ourselves what type of a relationship we have.''

Mac stood up and extended his hand toward Ty. "Fair enough.''

The two men shook hands, at first tentatively and then with the warmth resulting from years of friendship. A sense of relief washed through Ty. He still didn't know where his relationship with Angie was headed, but at least it would no longer exert a negative impact on his association with Mac. They could now give their attention and work energy to things that mattered to the future of the company.

Ty returned to his office to handle some reports he had shuffled aside while pursuing the incredibly desirable Angelina Coleman. But first, he placed a call to Angie. He wanted to share the news with her about he and Mac patching things up between them. He paused for a moment before dialing the last number. His first thought had been to share with Angie, to make her part of everything that was happening in his life. A warm flush of contentment quickly combined with a cold dash of uncertainty. He was in way over his head and didn't know what to do. He dialed the last number and listened as the phone rang.

"Did I wake you?'' The moment he heard her voice the warm flush of contentment won out.

"No, I've been up for over an hour.''

"I just wanted to let you know that Mac and I talked this morning and we have everything settled between us. How did you fare last night?''

"Mac and I talked half the night. We made a lot of progress in forging a new relationship between us—an adult relationship. It was the best talk we've ever had and it really felt good.''

"I'm glad. Listen, Angie... I just checked my calendar and I have a lunch meeting today that I had forgotten about so I'll be busy well into the afternoon. But, I'm free tonight." He dropped his voice to a low, almost conspiratorial whisper with just a hint of lusty desire attached to it. "Would you like to take another try at the hot tub?" He closed his eyes for a moment and allowed the memory of the bubbling water dancing over her bare breasts to play across the screen of his mind. His breathing quickened, forcing him to open his eyes and break the all too tempting image.

"Mmm...that sounds like a great idea."

"Good. I'll give you a call as I leave the office. Oh, I forgot to mention...this is swimsuit optional night."

"Does that apply to both of us?"

He heard the laughter in her voice and pictured her beautiful smile. It warmed his heart just to be talking to her. "Absolutely." He concluded the conversation, then turned his attention to work.

Ty couldn't stop his mind from wandering to the delights the evening had in store. His day seemed to drag by. He finally gave up trying to finish the reports and had to fight to keep his attention focused on his lunch meeting. The way she so totally occupied his thoughts when awake and his dreams when asleep left him perplexed at best. And at the worst, it left him scared out of his socks.

It also left him steeped in the type of turmoil that had never been a part of his life. It had always been so simple and straightforward. If a situation with a woman seemed to be cooling off, there were always several others available to heat things up again.

But this was so totally different. He didn't want to be with anyone else. He found himself trying to picture what it would be like twenty years from now when the hot passions had mellowed. He still couldn't imagine himself with anyone other than Angie.

He forced his attention back to work while keeping one eye on the clock. Closing time finally arrived. He called Angie to tell her he was on his way, then headed for his car. His heart sang and his spirits soared as he drove toward Mac's house. It was no use denying it. She had become the single most important person in his life. When they were apart it felt as if a piece of his life was missing.

But what to do about it? He tried to convince himself that he didn't need to do anything. What they had was perfect...well, *almost* perfect. It would be better when she wasn't staying with Mac. Once she moved out of Mac's house, they wouldn't need to be concerned about Mac's reaction if she stayed out all night.

Then his mind started to drift into very dangerous territory. He toyed with the idea of Angie moving in with him. But what kind of a message would that send to her? Would it signal his commitment to a relation-ship? Would it say even more than that? Was he ready to make that type of a statement? Again, the inner tur-moil started to churn in the pit of his stomach telling him how uncomfortable he was with the subject.

As soon as Angie opened the door he pulled her into his arms. It all felt so good, so right—so perfect. His turmoil stopped and in its place was the contentment and happiness he had come to associate with her, feel-ings he had never experienced with any other person.

Then his mouth was on hers. She circled her arms around his neck as their kiss deepened, sending yet another wave of desire crashing through his body. Did he dare acknowledge that he just might be falling in love with her? And if he were to consciously and openly deal with that reality, what would it mean for the future?

He banished the worrisome thoughts from his mind. Things between them were perfect just the way they were. They didn't need meaningless words to define what they had. They were good together and they belonged together. That was all that mattered.

He broke off the kiss, but continued to hold her in his arms. His whispered words held a breathless quality. "Have I ever told you how exquisitely marvelous you are?"

"No...at least not in those words."

"Then I've been neglectful in my duties." He captured her mouth with a tender kiss that spoke volumes in its emotion.

A few minutes later they were in his car driving toward his house. Champagne and the hot tub...even if they didn't make love, the evening would be ideal because he was spending it with Angie.

He pulled into the garage and they entered the house. Ty turned off the outside lights and disabled the motion lights on the deck so that everything was dark. The only illumination was the soft light filtering through from inside the house. He turned up the heat on the hot tub to raise the temperature to the proper level.

He retreated to his bedroom and emerged a few minutes later wearing a bathrobe. Angie waited in the den where she, too, was dressed in a bathrobe.

He held out his hand to her and gestured toward the deck. "Shall we?"

She took his hand. The loving squeeze he returned said as much as words. They went to the deck, dropped their robes and entered the bubbling water. She settled on the bench seat with Ty next to her. The water caressed her bare skin, stimulating her senses and warming her insides. She had never been nude in a hot tub before, just as she had never made love during the day or on a sailboat. The sensation of the swirling water against her completely naked body had an almost scandalous feel to it, one that heated her desires. Her life had been filled with several firsts since she had arrived from Portland.

Ty wrapped her in his arms and held her body tightly against his. He didn't seem to be able to keep his hands off her—the creamy smoothness of her skin, the scent of her perfume, delightful curves that would excite any man with a breath of life in him. He captured her mouth with a passion he couldn't keep hidden even if he wanted to. It was a mouth he couldn't get enough of, an addictive taste that always left him wanting more.

Everything about her had his sex drive running at full speed, but it wasn't the only thing about Angelina Coleman that he couldn't leave alone. There was the intelligent, compassionate, giving woman with the delicious sense of humor and the adventurous spirit who willingly embraced life, new experiences and the excitement life offered. He had never met anyone like her and knew he never would. She was unique and very special to him.

They stayed in the hot tub for a little over half an hour, then hand in hand retreated to his bedroom. Neither had said anything, yet they both knew what the culmination of the evening would be.

Ty allowed a quick thought about his life and future being solely in Angie's hands. His unspoken goal was to make her happy. But exactly what was it that would make her the happiest? What was the thing she wanted above all others? She had never mentioned it, but was commitment on that list? Would he ever be able to give her that one thing that she might want the most?

Eight

Ty entered the lobby at a little before eleven o'clock the next day. "Good morning, Ellen. Any phone messages for me?"

The receptionist handed him a stack of messages. "It seems that everyone's been looking for you this morning and almost all of them complained that you had your cell phone turned off."

He flashed a smile, one that said he was in an exceptionally good mood. "You can't make a multimillion-dollar presentation if your cell phone keeps interrupting."

"I take that to mean your presentation went well?"

"Very well."

Ty started across the lobby toward the hallway that led to the executive offices, then paused as he continued to shuffle through the numerous phone messages.

He stared at the written messages, but the words refused to register with him. His thoughts had deserted the business at hand and drifted to the previous night and Angie. As much as the idea frightened him, the word *love* continued to loom larger and larger in his consciousness.

The sound of someone entering the lobby drew his attention away from his thoughts. He turned to see a neatly dressed man of about thirty walk up to the reception desk.

Ty looked him over. The visitor seemed to be too stiff, had too much of an all-business attitude. He was too serious for Ty's liking. The aura of self-importance surrounding him grated against Ty's sensibilities.

"I want to see McConnor Coleman."

A jab of irritation poked at Ty. He hadn't asked to see Mac, he had demanded. Even the man's tone of voice sounded pompous. Something about this stranger's arrogant manner really rubbed him the wrong way. Hopefully the man wasn't a potential client. Anyone that uptight surely wouldn't be interested in owning a custom-designed sailboat. He decided to hang around the lobby long enough to find out who this man was and what brought him to their offices.

Ellen checked the appointment book, then looked up at the visitor. She gave him a questioning look cloaked in caution. "Do you have an appointment with Mr. Coleman?"

"No. This is a personal matter, not business. My name is Caufield Woodrow III."

A cold chill surged through Ty's body. *Caufield Woodrow III*...he had heard the name before. Mac had said it when he mentioned Angie's recently broken engagement. He looked the stranger over a little more carefully, almost in the same manner as the leader of the pack would size up the rival who was trying to usurp his position.

Every thought, every feeling, every spark of intuition racing around inside him told Ty this could not be good. Why would Angie's ex-fiancé need to be contacting Mac on a personal matter? And why would it require him to travel from Portland to Seattle to do it in person? Ty pretended to be shuffling through his phone messages, but his total attention became glued to the interaction between Ellen and this unwanted intruder.

"Mr. Coleman is in the lab right now. Would you care to wait? He should be back in his office shortly."

"I want you to page him now to let him know I'm here and want to see him immediately."

Ty clenched his jaw into a hard line. He noticed the way Ellen bristled at the man's attitude. He also noted her hesitation as she glanced in his direction as if asking what she should do. Ty stepped in to alleviate her concern and take control of the situation.

"I'm headed that way, Ellen. I'll let Mac know someone is here to see him." He made a subtle nod in her direction in response to her grateful smile. It was a short-lived moment, broken by the intruder's abrupt manner and take-charge attitude.

"I'm going with you."

Ty leveled a stern look at Caufield Woodrow III. His tone of voice was very no-nonsense, the words spoken in a matter-of-fact manner. "No, you aren't. We don't allow sightseers into the lab."

Caufield pulled himself up to his full height, about an inch shorter than Ty's six-foot frame. "I am a personal acquaintance of one of the owners and as such I—''

''And *I* am the other owner.'' There was nothing gracious in Ty's manner. ''I believe that supersedes your position. So, you can either sit and wait until Mac is free or you can make an appointment and come back at another time.'' Ty flashed his most polished smile, the one he reserved for dealing with unpleasant people. ''Whichever is more convenient for you.'' He saw the tension grip the visitor as his body stiffened.

Caufield clipped his words with his harsh reply. ''I'll wait.'' He made his way across the lobby to a couch and sat down.

Ty allowed an inner smile of satisfaction at having put this overbearing man in his place by making him back down. *I'm not about to allow you to bully your way into the inner workings of our company...and it would be the same even if you hadn't once been engaged to Angie.*

With that, Ty left the lobby and proceeded toward the lab. The anxiety pounded into him like nothing ever had before. What could Angie's ex-fiancé be doing there? Exactly which one of them was responsible for breaking off the engagement? Was Angie the one who made that decision or had the arrogant jerk he'd just encountered in the lobby been the one who hurt Angie by dumping her? A shiver of apprehension made its way through his body. Did she still have feelings for her ex-fiancé? Another twinge poked at Ty. If so, were they strong feelings?

Then he was forced to acknowledge the most painful thought of all. Would Caufield Woodrow III try to win Angie back? He shook his head. He had to get his rampaging thoughts under control. Perhaps Caufield's *personal matter* with Mac didn't have anything to do with Angie. Perhaps it was a business matter of some sort. A little tremor of anxiety told him that was only wishful thinking.

Ty quickly located Mac in the lab. "Sorry to interrupt your tests, but I thought you should know there's someone in the lobby to see you who is very impatient and unhappy about being kept waiting." He tried to project a nonchalant attitude, but knew he hadn't been very successful. "All in all a rather unpleasant man."

A slight frown crossed Mac's forehead, a frown that managed to convey both confusion and irritation at the interruption. "What are you talking about? I'm really busy here and don't have time to play guessing games."

"Caufield Woodrow III is what I'm talking about." He noted the look of surprise that darted across Mac's face. "He just marched in the front door and demanded to see you immediately on what he referred to as a *personal matter.*"

Mac straightened up and placed the file folder on the table next to the design model he'd been working on. "Caufield is here?"

"Yep…right out there in the lobby. Is he always that arrogant?"

"I…uh…really couldn't say. I've only been around him a couple of times. The first was at a party at his country club when he and Angie announced their engagement and the other occasion was a Christmas gathering at his family's house." A slight chuckle escaped his throat, one that did not really contain any humor. "House…we're talking a very large mansion with a full household staff. It's big bucks from old family money."

"And...uh..." Ty wasn't sure how to say what was on his mind or whether he should say it at all. "And it was Angie who broke off the engagement with him?"

"Hmm, I'm not sure how all of that happened or why. All I know is that she said the engagement was off."

Mac's answer did nothing to alleviate Ty's rapidly expanding anxiety. He still didn't know what happened between Angie and Caufield that resulted in breaking off the engagement. And he was afraid to ask her, afraid of what the answer might be—afraid it might have been Caufield who dumped Angie, leaving her carrying a torch for a lost love. All he knew was a man from Angie's past was in the lobby and he didn't like it. He also didn't like the strange feelings it produced— feelings that were foreign to him. He thoroughly resented this interloper.

An errant thought floated into his mind. Could the strange feeling be jealousy? He had no experience with jealousy in connection with any woman he had ever dated. Everything was always no-strings-attached. There was always another beautiful and willing companion waiting in the wings. But this was an entirely different sensation...foreign...uncomfortable. He didn't like these feelings and especially didn't like what they were trying to tell him—that Angie was far more important to him than he had been willing to admit. That maybe the word *love* was more appropriate than he wanted it to be. He tried to shove the worries from his mind as he turned his attention to Mac.

"Well? Are you going to leave him sitting there?"

Mac sighed. "I suppose I should go and see what he wants, but he sure showed up at an inconvenient time for me. I'm just too busy to become involved in whatever is on his mind."

"I'll be happy to handle it for you." Ty attempted to control the gleeful rush at the prospect of being able to put a quick stop to whatever Caufield had come to do and get him headed back toward Portland before Angie even knew he was in town. His upbeat moment disappeared as quickly as it had materialized. What would Angie's reaction be if she found out he had sent her ex-fiancé packing without even telling her Caufield had come to see her brother? He shook his head in resignation. He couldn't do that. He didn't have the right to make that decision for her or interfere in her life in that manner.

"No, I'll handle it. I'll be there in a couple of minutes, as soon as I get this model put away." Mac returned his attention to what he had been doing before Ty interrupted him.

Ty went to his office, making sure his door was wide open so he would know when Mac and Caufield went to Mac's office. It's not that he planned to eavesdrop on them, but if their conversation just happened to filter into his office...

The sound of Mac's voice moving down the hallway toward the office interrupted his thoughts.

"I must say, Caufield, this is a surprise. I wish you would have called so I could have rearranged my schedule."

"This was the only available time I had."

Ty heard it in Caufield's voice, the attitude that said his was the only valuable time, not anyone else's— everyone had to accommodate his schedule.

Mac's words were clipped, his attitude brusque. "That's too bad because right now I only have a few minutes to give you. Whatever it is that's so important you felt the need to demand to speak to me immediately…well, I suggest you start talking and make it quick.''

Ty moved away from his office door as the two men drew closer, but he stayed within hearing range. It was obvious that Mac did not particularly care for Caufield, but Ty didn't know why. He did know that it gave him a surge of satisfaction, vindication for his own feelings toward someone he really didn't know. As soon as Mac and Caufield entered Mac's office, Ty stationed himself next to the office door and continued to listen while ignoring his feelings of guilt.

''All right, Caufield. What's up?''

''I'm told Angelina is here, that she's staying with you.''

''Yes, she's staying with me. Now, is that all you wanted? To verify her whereabouts?''

''Not at all. I'm here to take her back to Portland with me. I've allowed her this bit of time to get over her pre-wedding jitters, but now she needs to return so we can complete our wedding plans.''

''That's odd. Angie didn't say anything to me about returning to Portland. I'm under the impression that she intends to stay in Seattle, get a job and find her own place to live.''

''Not at all. I'll admit that we had a little tiff, but nothing serious. She'll be returning to Portland with me. Now, I need your address so that I can collect her. I'll send for her belongings and car when we get back to Portland.''

The words rang in Ty's ears. *Complete our wedding plans…she'll be returning to Portland with me.* It felt as if someone had landed a solid punch to his solar plexus. A sudden rush of fear burned in his throat. He strained to listen, but didn't hear anything. They had stopped talking, but what could they be doing? Was Mac writing down his address to give it to Caufield? Why didn't Mac just tell the arrogant jerk to take a hike? If Angie wanted to return to Portland she would do it on her own. She didn't need someone to *collect* her.

If Angie wanted to return…suddenly all the wind went out of his sails, his indignation and determination faltered. *If*…only two letters, but such a powerful word.

Ty didn't know what to think or what to do. He took a calming breath hoping it would help, but it didn't. A sick feeling welled inside him. The possibilities forced their way into his thoughts, possibilities that he didn't want to think about.

Mac's voice broke into Ty's mounting panic as the conversation from the next office resumed.

"Here's my address."

"I want you to call Angelina and let her know I'm on my way so she can be ready to go when I arrive."

"Sorry, Caufield. I've just given you all the time I can spare. As I said, you should have called and made an appointment."

A moment later Ty saw Mac usher Caufield toward the lobby, then Mac returned to the lab. Mac's actions sent a little ripple of satisfaction pushing its way through Ty's body. There was no doubt in his mind that Mac did not like Caufield Woodrow III.

He hurried to the lab, catching up with Mac at the door. "So, what was that all about?"

"That was Angie's ex-fiancé. He says he came here to escort her back to Portland so they can get married."

The trepidation filled Ty's voice attesting to his less-than-calm state of mind. "And you're just going to let him do it?"

Mac leveled a steady look at Ty. "Correct me if I'm wrong, but haven't I been told in no uncertain terms by both you and Angie that she is an adult and can speak for herself and make her own mature decisions? This is between Caufield and Angie. It's not for me to decide what's best for her. It's her decision."

Mac returned to the project he had been working on when Caufield arrived, leaving Ty standing there wondering what to say or do in response to Mac's statement. He shook his head in resignation as he admitted there was nothing he could say. Mac had been right in not interfering, but it didn't make Ty feel any better.

Ty returned to his office. Maybe he should drive over to Mac's house as if he was unaware of Caufield being there. He shook his head in disgust. It was a lousy idea. But knowing what the right thing was and being happy with the decision were two entirely different matters. Yep, rushing to Mac's house would definitely be a bad idea. And knowing that her ex-fiancé had arrived on the scene to take her back to Portland so they could be married did not make that decision any easier to accept.

He had a date with Angie that evening, as he had almost every night since her arrival. They had planned to go to the art gallery they had missed the night they first made love. He would pick her up as they had planned. They had something very special between them, something that couldn't be shaken by the arrival of a former lover.

A little scowl wrinkled across Ty's forehead as an unwanted thought invaded his logic. Caufield Woodrow III was more than a former lover. He was her ex-fiancé. He was a man who had not been afraid to make a commitment to their relationship.

A man who had asked her to marry him—a man who willingly sought out marriage—was a difficult thing to battle. It was the type of competition Ty had never been involved with. A little shudder of trepidation made its way through his body. He wasn't at all sure what the hours ahead would bring.

Ty returned to his office and tried to concentrate on work, but it was an impossible task. Angie consumed his thoughts, his energy and his very existence. What would happen when Caufield reached Mac's house? Maybe Angie wouldn't be there. The thought bright-ened his mood, but only for a second or two. Caufield didn't seem like the type who would be dissuaded that easily, not when he had driven from Portland for the single-minded purpose of taking Angie back with him.

''Caufield!'' The shock spread through Angie when she opened the door and saw him standing on the porch. She remained frozen to the spot, unable to move. She finally managed to force out a few more words. ''What are you doing here?''

''May I come in, Angelina? I'd prefer to discuss our business inside rather than out here on the porch.''

''Uh…yes, of course.'' She stepped aside as he en-tered the house. ''You said you were here to discuss business of some sort? What business do we have that would bring you to Seattle?''

He extended a smile. ''Is that fresh coffee I smell?''

The initial shock of seeing him had worn off to be quickly replaced by a ripple of irritation. She was well acquainted with Caufield's stalling tactics when he wanted to control things and force events into his pre-determined schedule. His fresh coffee comment was just such a tactic.

"Yes, I just made some." She didn't offer him anything, not even a chair.

"Do you suppose I could have a cup?" He looked around the room. "And maybe sit down for a bit? I've just had a long drive from Portland and am a little weary."

Angie gestured toward a chair, then disappeared into the kitchen. Her irritation level increased. *Long drive from Portland.* What an absurd thing for him to say. Did he really think she wasn't aware of the fact that Portland to Seattle was less than a three-hour drive and it was Interstate highway the entire distance?

She returned to the living room a minute later carrying a mug of hot coffee which she handed to him. Caufield had seated himself on the sofa, so she purposely chose a chair on the other side of the coffee table.

"Thank you, Angelina dear." He took a sip from the cup, then set it on the coffee table.

Angelina dear. It had such a condescending sound to it, one that grated on her nerves. At first it hadn't bothered her all that much, but as the end of their relationship became apparent she found it more and more annoying.

"I would appreciate it if you would stop calling me that."

He cocked his head and looked at her for a moment as if trying to figure out what she was talking about. "Calling you what, Angelina dear? If I've done something to offend you, then I'm truly sorry."

There it was again. He was patronizing her. "My

name is Angelina, not Angelina dear. Actually, I prefer Angie to Angelina.''

''No, no—Angie sounds so…I don't know…so common. I much prefer your given name—Angelina, as in Angel.''

She attempted to suppress the sigh of resignation that forced its way out into the open. There was nothing to be gained by pursuing that line of conversation. ''Why are you here, Caufield?''

''I thought that would have been obvious. I'm here to take you back to Portland with me so we can be married, just as we planned. There are lots of preparations that need to be tended to. Mother has already booked the country club for the reception following the ceremony and has set the menu. She wants you to wear her wedding dress. She made an appointment for you next Monday with her dressmaker to make the necessary alterations.''

There it was again. He had made all her decisions about the wedding, even down to the dress she would wear. His family had taken over the planning of everything even though it was supposed to be the bride's decision. He was still attempting to suffocate her with his total control over every facet of her life.

And there was no way she would ever allow that to happen again.

''You seem to be confused, Caufield. Please listen carefully to what I'm about to say. We are no longer engaged. We are not getting married. I won't be going back to Portland with you. I don't know how much clearer I can be.''

''Now, Angelina…I understand about pre-wedding jitters. You're feeling a little scared right now, which is certainly normal. But everything will be perfect. I can provide you with whatever you want. You won't need to ever work again. I've already purchased our house and have Mother's interior decorator ordering the furnishings. You're going to love it.''

"Caufield—'' Her voice rose in anger. "Why can't you get it through your head that I don't love you and will not be marrying you?''

"That's nonsense. However, I can see that we won't be returning to Portland today. I'm going to check into the Four Seasons Hotel in Seattle. We can leave tomorrow if that's more convenient for you.''

He paused to take a drink of his coffee. "Now that we have that settled, tell me what you have been doing since you've been here.''

He had done it to her again. How typical of Caufield. He had dismissed her comments as if they had no relevance to anything. Then he had moved on by adopting the air of someone interested in her activities. Somehow she didn't think he would really want to know exactly what she had been doing since her arrival at her brother's house. And exactly what had that been?

She had fallen in love with the most incredible man she had ever met—lover, charmer, caring companion...someone who listened to her and expressed a genuine interest in her likes and dislikes. She had established a brand-new relationship with her brother. She had never felt so alive and excited about what the future held.

Somehow she had to make Caufield listen to her, to accept that they were through. Maybe if she approached the problem from a different angle. She sat on the couch next to him and spoke softly, trying to make each word sound as sincere as it truly was.

"Caufield...you have a lot to offer to the right

woman, but I'm not that woman.'' She made eye contact with him, holding his gaze. ''I could never be happy living the type of life you offer, nor could I be the kind of wife that you want. You deserve someone who will love you all-out and want the same things from life that you do. I'm not that person.''

''Of course you are. How could anyone not want everything I have to offer and I'm offering it all to you on a silver platter.''

''No, you're offering me what you think is the ideal relationship. You've never bothered to find out what it is that I want from a relationship or what I want out of life. I'm afraid your silver platter has too many strings attached to it.'' *Not the least of which is your overbearing mother.* It was certainly no mystery where he learned to be so controlling or why his father had finally thrown his hands up in the air, said goodbye and walked out the door never to be seen again. ''There can't be a marriage without love.''

His voice was very matter-of-fact, without any real emotion attached to it. ''I love you, Angelina, and you love me. You said so when we became engaged.''

''I thought I did, but I later realized that you had overwhelmed me with your dazzling courtship. Once my head came down from the clouds I knew I needed to live in reality, not on some ivory pedestal built to your specifications.''

Caufield's gaze shifted around the room, then came to rest on his coffee mug. ''I see that I haven't given you quite enough time to get this out of your system.'' He rose to his feet, placed his hands on her shoulders and stared at her for a moment. ''As I said, I'll be checking into the Four Seasons. We'll talk again tomorrow. You'll ride back to Portland with me. I'll send someone for your car.''

Her exasperation finally won out. She had been truthful. She had been kind. She had been straightforward and honest. Nothing had worked. ''I've tried everything I know, but you refuse to listen.''

''I heard every word you've said and I—''

''You may have heard every word, but you're not listening to what I'm saying. There is nothing left to talk about. Please leave.''

''I'll stay in Seattle for two more days. I expect to hear from you tomorrow.'' He leaned forward to kiss her, but she pulled back.

''Goodbye, Caufield. I won't be calling you. I wish you luck in finding the type of woman you're looking for.''

Angie escorted him to the front door and watched as he drove away. Hopefully that chapter of her life had finally been closed for good. But what did the next chapter hold? Caufield had professed his love, committed to a relationship and wanted her to marry him. Ty, on the other hand, had not offered any type of a commitment, had not told her he loved her and certainly had not discussed what their future together might be.

A shadow of foreboding settled across her thoughts. Exactly what type of relationship did she and Ty have? And where was it headed? Or more specifically, was it headed anywhere at all? It seemed as if she had asked herself those questions several times a day, but had never been able to settle on a definitive answer. The confusion and the unanswered questions were never very far from the forefront of her mind. Would they ever be anything more than just lovers? Was it a relationship doomed to failure?

Angie tried to dismiss her concerns by busying herself with a project. She had neglected her original goal while basking in the delicious attentions of Tyler Farrell. It had been a true whirlwind encounter, but her confrontation with Caufield had dramatically yanked her back to reality. She had chosen to be the master of her own destiny and fate. It was up to her to build for the future. She loved Ty, but it took more than a one-sided love to make a future that would last a lifetime. She had to be practical, not live on hopes and dreams of what a future with him could be.

And the first order of business she needed to address was to stop sponging off her brother and find a place of her own to live. She grabbed the morning newspaper and turned to the classified ads. She passed the rest of the afternoon checking the rentals, circling several in Seattle, a couple on Bainbridge Island and one on Mercer Island. Then almost as an afterthought she looked at the help wanted ads. She had been pinning her hopes on a career position with Mac's company, but now she wondered if that was really the most practical route for her to pursue.

It wouldn't do any harm to check the job market, see what type of positions were available. She was both surprised and pleased to see several ads looking for someone with her qualifications. She circled those, too. She chose not to dwell on what might have prompted her to check the job situation. Perhaps her single-minded goal wasn't as set as she thought it was. Another little twinge of foreboding swept through her, trying to tell her something she did not want to know.

Nine

Angie glanced at the clock and was surprised to see how late it was. She had been looking over the classified ads longer than she realized. Ty would be picking her up in an hour and she needed to get ready. Another tickle of discomfort poked at her. Caufield's visit had shaken her up more than she first realized, but perhaps some good had resulted from it. She had come back down to earth again and refocused on her goal.

She took a quick shower, put on her makeup and dressed for her date. She pulled the last stroke of her brush through her hair just as the doorbell rang. A surge of excitement hit her. Just knowing that Ty was on the other side of the door filled her with joy. She rushed to open the door, to once again be with him. She wanted to erase her confrontation with Caufield from her mind.

The moment she opened the door Ty pulled her into

his arms. He had been on edge all afternoon, wrestling with the concept of jealousy. The only thing he wanted was to hold her, to feel her warmth and savor her closeness. It all felt so right. The unexpected arrival of her ex-fiancé had thrown him for a loop. It was the type of opposition he didn't know how to deal with—a man who had offered a commitment to a relationship and marriage to the woman he didn't want to lose.

He had not seen any strange cars parked in the driveway or in front of Mac's house. He glanced from the entryway into the living room, but didn't see anyone. Nervous energy welled inside him as he cleared his throat.

"You...uh, you're alone?"

"Yes. Who did you expect to find?"

"Uh...well, I was at the office when...uh, Mac mentioned that your—"

"Oh, you're talking about Caufield."

"He's...uh..." Ty looked around the living room again. "He's gone back to Portland?"

"No, at least not right away. He's checking into a hotel in Seattle for a day or two."

"Oh...I see." He knew the disappointment had crept into his voice, but he had not been able to prevent it. The emotion had been too strong, the stakes too high. At that moment he felt totally out of control, incapable of rational thought. He desperately needed to rein in his anxieties and fears.

"He showed up here this afternoon. It was quite a surprise to me." A twinge of trepidation pushed at her. She had hoped to escape any conversation about Caufield, but that apparently wasn't going to happen. "I had no idea he was in town."

"He's here on business? Perhaps a couple of days

vacation and decided to stop by to say hello as long as he was in the area?'' Ty knew he was grasping at straws, but couldn't banish the anguish that refused to let go of him. He desperately needed some reassurances that his fears were groundless.

Angie drew in a calming breath. There didn't seem to be any way out of it other than to meet his questions head-on. "No. He came specifically to see me. He wants me to return to Portland with him so we can be married.'' There…she had said it. And she didn't want to discuss it any further. As far as she was concerned, Caufield Woodrow III was a closed subject.

She looked up at him. "Could we drop it now?''

"Certainly. I didn't mean to sound like I was prying into your personal business. It's just that…uh…'' He glanced at his watch. He didn't like the uneasiness that surrounded him, a discomfort that he knew was directly attributable to the arrival of her ex-fiancé. "We'd better be going. We have to hurry or we'll miss the ferry and have to wait for the next one.''

"I'll get my purse and jacket.'' She retreated to the bedroom.

Angie sat on the edge of the bed as she tried to collect her composure. She knew her tone of voice had been a little sharp, but Caufield's visit had unnerved her and then to have Ty question her about it…well, it had set her on edge a little.

The dark cloud of foreboding settled over her again. Everything had been so marvelous since her arrival at Mac's house. Only now she had been hit with the awareness that what she thought was on the way to being her perfect world had started to crumble. She wasn't sure what to make of the unsettled feeling and didn't know what to do to stop it. She tried to dismiss

it by assuring herself that it was just the sudden and
unexpected appearance of Caufield that had set her
nerves on edge. There was nothing wrong. Caufield
would return to Portland and she and Ty would continue. A little furrow wrinkled across her forehead. But
continue what? What did they have and where was it
going?

She took a calming breath. There it was again…the
same questions about the future of her relationship with
Ty. She gathered her things and returned to the living
room where he was waiting. ''I'm ready. Shall we
go?'' She extended a smile, one she hoped would tell
him that everything was all right, nothing between
them had changed.

But it was far from the truth. Nothing was all right
and she didn't know what to do to fix it. Or if it could
even be fixed. She loved Ty, but she didn't have a clue
what was going on in his mind. Even the unexpected
arrival of Caufield and her comment about him wanting
her to return to Portland so they could be married had
not moved Ty to say anything or offer anything.

The last thing she wanted to do was force Ty into a
commitment he didn't want, but she needed to know
where things stood between them. She wanted to know
what the future held and where she was headed. She
needed some sort of reassurance from him, even if it
was only to know that they had reached the limit of
what could be. But as much as she wanted to know,
she was afraid of where that might be. And the fear
continued to eat at her.

Ty and Angie drove off the ferry at Bainbridge Island. He steered directly toward his house as if it was
the most natural thing to be doing. The anxiety of ear-

lier that evening had moved away and the comfort and closeness he had come to associate with Angie had returned. He had been foolish to allow his fears and assumptions to grow to such proportions. Everything was terrific, just as it had been before the arrival of her ex-fiancé.

He gave her hand a little squeeze. "What did you think of the gallery?"

"I'm not sure. They had some nice pieces and paintings, but most of the items they displayed were a little bit too avant-garde for my tastes. What did you think?"

"I thought so, too. It was interesting, but not what I would want displayed in my home." He wanted to put his arm around her shoulder, but bucket seats didn't allow for that type of intimacy. Instead he had to be content with clasping her hand in his. He had been tense earlier that evening and he knew exactly why—Caufield Woodrow III. He had not been happy with Angie's answer that Caufield had checked into a hotel in Seattle rather than returning to Portland. She had also been very clear about Caufield's intentions in being at Mac's house, that he wanted her to return to Portland with him so they could be married.

Ty had tried to put it out of his mind. The bottom line was that Caufield had left Bainbridge Island and Angie was with him rather than Caufield. She hadn't even brought it up for discussion or asked him anything about the future. Since she had chosen to be with him rather than her ex-fiancé it had to mean she was happy with their relationship just as it was, regardless of Caufield's willingness to make a commitment and even propose to her.

Ty fought to make that assumption a reality. They didn't need any verbal promises to know how they felt about each other. Things were perfect just as they were. That was what he wanted to believe, what he *needed* to believe. If nothing else, it eased his mind about the problem of verbalizing a commitment to the relationship. The words were not necessary. They both knew what they shared without talking about it.

Angie gazed out the window. "You missed the turn-off for Mac's house."

"It's still early. I thought we could get something to eat at my house and maybe catch the late news on television." He squeezed her hand and shot a sideways grin toward her. "Is that okay with you?"

"That sounds great." He hadn't turned loose of her hand since they drove off the ferry. His reassuring touch provided a sensual warmth that cut through her earlier anxieties. As long as they were together, why was a verbal commitment so important? Did a few words really make a difference to the feeling and emotion that bound them together?

She wanted to believe that it didn't matter, but deep down inside she knew it did. She knew she couldn't live her life as nothing more than someone's lover, even someone as dynamic as Tyler Farrell. She had to have some type of reassurance about his feelings and their future. Was that wanting more than was possible? More than Ty was willing to give? It was a concern that continued to grow larger and more worrisome with each passing day, no matter how much she tried to convince herself that it wasn't important.

Ty pulled into his garage and they entered the house through the kitchen. He kept up a light patter of conversation. "Let's see what's in the refrigerator that will be quick and easy." He moved a few things around as he surveyed the contents. "I have the makings of a salad. Let me check the freezer. Maybe there's something we can pop into the microwave.''

He paused a moment, then pulled her into his embrace. The emotion overwhelmed him as he delved into the depths of her eyes. Visions of Caufield Woodrow III continued to circulate through his mind. How close had he come to losing her to this rival from her past? A cold shudder told him how painful the thought was.

''I'm really not very hungry. How about you?'' Once again the warmth of her body and the closeness of her very existence filled him with a sense of well-being, contentment and the type of fulfillment and completion that had never been part of his life until he met Angie. It was the type of happiness he had never known, one that nearly overpowered everything else in his life. He lowered his mouth to hers, the kiss tender and sweet. He reveled in the moment. He wanted her to be part of his life forever.

Once again a sense of relief washed through him. Caufield had gone. There was a very nice motel on Bainbridge Island yet Caufield had chosen to leave the island rather than check in there. His rival for her affections was no longer in the picture.

She broke the kiss, leaning her head back slightly. A little smile tugged at the corners of her mouth. ''I'm not very hungry, either.''

He caressed her shoulders, then brushed a loving kiss across her lips. ''Perhaps we can find something else to do.''

He took her hand as they walked toward his bedroom. No words were spoken. They weren't necessary. A few minutes later they snuggled together in the comfort of his king-size bed, bare skin pressing against bare skin. For several minutes they simply held each other, content to be wrapped in the warmth that enveloped them.

He caressed her shoulders, lightly brushed his fingertips across her smooth skin, then ran his fingers through her hair as he cradled her head against his shoulder. More than anything he wanted Angie by his side for the rest of his life. He wanted to wake up each morning and find her next to him. A moment of doubt tried to invade his consciousness, but he quickly shoved it away. With Caufield now out of the picture he knew everything would be all right. There was no need to discuss him any further, no need to worry about a rival. All his attentions and energy could be directed to Angie. His mouth found hers, the addictive taste he could not get enough of and the woman he never wanted to lose.

The moment his lips touched hers any and all thoughts, doubts and fears disappeared from Angie's mind. She ran her hands across his muscled chest, broad shoulders and back. She loved him so very much. She never realized what true love was until Tyler Farrell became part of her life.

They made love—slowly, sensually and completely. It was different than the other times. The heated passion of hormones took a back seat to the caring and emotion that passed between them. She had never felt so whole...so complete. It was as if all the missing pieces of her life had at last been found.

They remained wrapped in each other's arms, quietly savoring the afterglow and togetherness. Every few minutes he placed a tender kiss on her forehead or cheek and stroked the creamy smoothness of her skin. It was a time of emotional intimacy, closeness and caring.

But for Angie it was more. It had an almost bitter-sweet feel to it as if they were saying goodbye. As warm and happy as she was, she couldn't stop her mind from wandering to the concern that had grown from a mere errant thought to a worry that grew larger and more formidable with each passing day. She needed his reassurance that they had a future together. She needed to have her uneasiness settled once and for all.

Ty pulled her tighter into his embrace. She didn't know if he was asleep or not, but being in his arms felt so good, so right. It was a place she wanted to spend the rest of her life. Again the dark cloud of fore-boding drifted across her mind, blocking out the warmth. As much as she tried to tell herself that she didn't need any more of a commitment from him than what his actions displayed, she knew it was nothing more than hollow words.

She continued to snuggle in his arms, but the contentment of earlier ebbed away to be replaced by doubts and confusion about how to handle the situation. She had arrived in Seattle with a definite goal in mind and a determination to achieve that goal. Her resolve and her goal had slipped away and she needed to get it back. If Ty would only do something, give her some kind of indication about their future—any type of a sign.

But Ty did nothing to reassure her. He held her, he stroked her hair and skin, he gave her his warmth and tenderness, but he did not give her the words she wanted to hear—the words she *needed* to hear.

The hour grew later. Angie slid out of bed to get dressed. She couldn't stay all night at Ty's house. She may have forged a new adult relationship with her brother, but she knew staying overnight at Ty's house was not something Mac would accept. Besides, she needed some time alone to think—to work out what to do.

Ty reached out and grabbed her hand. "It's not that late. Do you really need to leave?" He squeezed her hand as he looked hopefully into her eyes. "I don't want you to go."

"I have several things to do in the morning. Besides, I should be considerate of Mac's feelings as long as I'm staying at his house. I can't be running in and out at all hours of the night."

"You don't have to stay at Mac's house." He paused for a moment, his words hesitant. "You can stay here."

"I can't casually sleep over here sometimes and then be at Mac's house sometimes." She looked at him, trying to read the unspoken words in his eyes. "I need somewhere permanent—someplace where I can unpack my clothes and know that's where they belong...where *I* belong. I need to know what the future holds."

She held her breath, hoping against hope that he would say more, that he would tell her why he didn't want her to leave his house. That he would make some sort of commitment and give her that place where she would belong.

But he didn't say anything else. Her hopes had been dashed, her fears had been valid, her unasked questions had now been answered. By his silence he had made it clear that this was the limit of their relationship. This was all it would ever be. The sorrow welled inside her, the pain she didn't think she would ever experience had wormed its way into her consciousness and it was worse than she feared it might be.

She mustered a weak smile. ''I really do need to leave.''

She had to leave—to leave Mac's house and find a place of her own, to leave her original job goal and find a new one, to leave Bainbridge Island and to leave a dead-end relationship with the man she loved more than she thought possible. Yes...she needed to leave for her own well-being. But would she be able to muster the courage to do it?

Ty dressed and drove her to Mac's house. He walked her to the door. ''Will I see you tomorrow night?''

''I'm not sure. I've been shamefully neglecting my own business and need to do some catching up.'' The words had been difficult for her to say, but she knew she had to start the separation process if she ever hoped to get on with her life. She saw the hint of confusion dart across his features and she felt herself weaken in her determination.

''I'll call you tomorrow afternoon.'' He kissed her tenderly on the lips, then returned to his car.

Angie continued to watch until his car was out of sight, all the while her sorrow growing to greater proportions. Not in her wildest imagination had she ever believed it would end this way—not with a fight, not with an explosion, not with an emotional outburst or upheaval. It was a quiet decision—her decision that she couldn't continue a relationship that was one-sided regardless of how much she loved him.

Ty knew her ex-fiancé had made a special trip to Bainbridge Island to see her and take her back to Portland with him. Somehow she had hoped he would at least express some concern that she might be thinking about a return to Caufield, but he hadn't shown any trepidation about the possibility that she might be considering her ex-fiancé's offer. She told Ty she needed to have some place she knew was permanent, to know where she belonged. She told him she needed reassurance about the future. He hadn't offered her what she had asked for.

It was obvious that as far as he was concerned everything was fine just the way it was. But she couldn't live with that. She needed more. She needed that commitment to the future.

She needed to know that he loved her.

Caufield's unexpected visit had forced two major decisions for Angie. The first was wanting Ty to say something that would define their relationship, but he had not provided her with that. And the second was realizing her career and future didn't depend on procuring a job with Mac's company. In retrospect she saw what a bad idea it had been all along. She would never be the independent career woman she wanted to be as long as she continued to tie her future to her brother.

The heavy weight of despair settled on her shoulders. A heartbroken Angie went inside the house, undressed and sank into the bed. Her thoughts and fears continued to swirl around in her head, feeding her distress and giving her a fitful night and very little sleep. Daylight invaded the bedroom before she was ready for it. She reluctantly dragged herself out of bed.

Even though her restless night had not provided her with very much sleep, it had given her an answer to her dilemma and a direction for the future. The only thing for her to do was to make a clean break of everything and step into the unknown on her own two feet. Ty had not shown any signs of being tired of their relationship or wanting to end it in any way, but she could not continue living in a vacuum—some sort of middle ground where she didn't know.

She knew what had to be done and even though it pained her, she had to do it. She showered, dressed and went to the kitchen where she found Mac making coffee.

He turned around when she entered the room and flashed a warm smile in her direction. "Good morning, Angie. There will be fresh coffee in just a few minutes." He took the carton from the refrigerator and poured two glasses of orange juice, handing one of them to her.

Angie took the glass, but set it on the counter without taking a drink. "Do you have a little bit of time before you go to work?"

Mac placed his glass on the counter. He shot her a quizzical look. "Is there something wrong?"

She gathered her determination. "I need to leave Bainbridge Island—today."

Mac's expression changed to one of shock followed by deep concern. "I've got as much time as you want." He pulled out a chair from the kitchen table for her, then sat down on the other side of the table facing her. "Why this sudden decision to leave?"

"It's not all that sudden, it's been brewing for a while. I have to get on with my life. I'm only kidding myself by thinking that my future is here. I left Portland to start a new life, to have a career. I thought working for you would be my answer. I could show you that I was capable and forge a career with your company."

"It was a good plan. With our expansion there will be a lot of restructuring within the company and you'll fit right in. It will definitely be something that is a career rather than just a job.''

''But don't you see, Mac? It's not really a feasible plan at all. I would once again be depending on you to provide for me.''

''Don't be ridiculous. I would expect you to earn your money just like any other employee.''

''That's not the point. I've given this a lot of thought. It would still be you giving me the job rather than hiring someone else who might be more qualified or have more experience even though I would be capable of handling the work.''

Mac wrinkled his brow into a slight frown as he stood up. He reached for the coffeepot and poured two cups, placing one of them in front of Angie. He cocked his head and stared at her for a moment, then sat down. ''What's really going on here, Angie? I hear what you're saying, but I don't believe what I'm hearing. There's more to this decision of yours than what you're telling me.''

She nervously played with her coffee cup then took a sip, but was unable to make eye contact with him. ''I...uh...I don't know what you mean.''

''Angie? What's really wrong?''

She finally looked up at her brother. She saw the deep concern etched into his handsome features. But after that grand speech she had made where she informed him she was an adult and capable of making her own decisions...well, how could she share her real feelings about her less-than-firm convictions concerning her current situation. It would be like admitting defeat, confessing that she wasn't as mature and capable as she thought.

She tried to rally her determination. It was her mess.

She had made it and it was up to her to fix it. She had done the one thing she swore she wouldn't do—she had become involved with another man and fallen in love. The man she had fallen in love with was very different from her ex-fiancé, but he was as wrong for her as Caufield had been.

Mac had been right. She and Ty lived in two different worlds and Ty's world moved in the fast lane of living for the moment with no commitments to a relationship or to the future. She had tried, had told herself it didn't matter, but in the end it was something she couldn't live with.

Now it was time for her to move on and put her life in order.

"Angie?"

Mac's voice drew her out of her thoughts. "I'll pack my things and take the ferry to Seattle this afternoon. I can get a motel room until I find a place to live. I've already circled several apartment possibilities in the newspaper and have checked the help wanted ads. There were some jobs listed in my area of expertise. I'll also sign up with a placement service. I'm sure I'll be able to find a job without any problem."

"That's ridiculous. There's absolutely no reason for you to pay for a motel room in Seattle. Even if you have your mind made up about getting a job elsewhere, there's no reason for you to leave my house and spend money on a motel. People commute to their jobs in Seattle every day from Bainbridge Island and the Olympic Peninsula. The ferry runs approximately every thirty minutes during the peak travel times on weekday mornings and evenings."

"You don't understand, Mac."

An audible sigh of resignation escaped his throat. "It

certainly isn't the first time that I haven't understood. What am I missing? Why do you feel you need to leave my house? Is it something I've done? Something I haven't done? Something I've said? Something I should have said? What is it?''

"No, you've been terrific just like you always are. It's just that…well…'' She nervously shifted her weight in her chair as she desperately searched for the right words, then finally blurted out what had been there all along. "I can't stay here where I'll be running into Ty all the time. I need to distance myself from him so that I can get on with my life.''

Mac's anger rose in his voice. "Did he do something to hurt you? Did he take advantage of you?''

"No! Calm down, Mac. It's nothing like that.'' How was she going to explain things to Mac without him jumping to the wrong conclusion? "I can't stay here any longer. It's obvious that Ty doesn't care as much about me as I do about him. I don't even know how or exactly when it happened. I didn't have any intention of becoming involved with someone after breaking off with Caufield, but somehow it just happened. Ty didn't do anything wrong. He's probably not even aware of how I feel. But I think, for my own well-being, that I should leave here. I need to find a job and make a life of my own. I need for it to be my life once again.''

She looked at her brother, her voice almost pleading. "You do understand, don't you?''

He shook his head as he furrowed his brow in confusion. "I had no idea you…I knew you and Ty had been spending a lot of time together, but I guess I was so wrapped up in my design project that I didn't realize just how much time that was. I didn't know things had gone so far, that you had become…'' He reached across the table, took her hand in his and gave it a loving brotherly squeeze. ''You really do care a great deal about him, don't you?''

Angie's voice had become a soft whisper. A sob caught in her throat as she spoke. ''More than I believed could be possible.''

''What can I do to help you? What do you need from me?''

Angie rose from her chair, came around the table and gave Mac a hug. ''You've already done it by just being here. It's my problem and I'll handle it.'' Her words may have been brave and self-assured, but inside she was a mass of quivering insecurities enveloped in an almost overwhelming sadness. She knew she would never love anyone as much as she loved Tyler Farrell, but she knew a one-sided love had no future to it.

''How are you fixed for money? It's going to cost you to live in a motel until you find an apartment and then whatever you rent will require deposits in addition to the rent.''

''Money is not a problem. I've saved and have a good cushion to fall back on until I start generating an income. I'll be fine.''

''Are you sure? I'll be happy to give—''

''No more handouts, Mac.''

''Okay…I'll be happy to *lend* you some money until you get a job. You can pay it back whenever it's convenient. Is that better?''

She gave him a warm smile. ''It's better, but not necessary. I'll be fine, honest.''

''Are you determined to do this?''

''Yes. I've given this a lot of thought and it's the best thing for me to do.''

"Okay. I'm not happy, but I'll respect your decision. Just one thing—you call me as soon as you get checked into a motel so I'll know where you are."

"Of course I will. I'm not running away and trying to hide so no one will know where I am. I just have to make this break and get my life back on track again. I appreciate all that you've done for me and am grateful for having this place to stay."

"I can certainly understand you wanting to find your own place to live, but there's still no reason why you couldn't work for the company. It would be a good career and a job where you could earn your own way."

He offered a tentative smile. "I promise not to give you any special treatment."

She returned a teasing smile. "Well, what good would it do to work for my brother if I couldn't take advantage and get special privileges?" The smile quickly faded and her voice fell off to a near whisper as she glanced at the floor. "Besides, it wouldn't work, not with Ty being there all the time." She saw the muscles tense in Mac's face in response to her statement.

They continued to talk during breakfast. Angie didn't bring up the subject of Ty and to her surprise, neither did Mac. She was grateful that he had apparently decided to accept her explanation without trying to dig out more information. She had already said more than she originally intended to. She told Mac she would call him before leaving his house to catch the ferry.

Once Mac had left for work, she set about packing up everything she had brought with her and loading up her car for her move. Every few minutes a wave of anguish hit her, accompanied by doubts and confusion. Was she really doing the right thing? Should she say something to Ty? Give him yet another chance to offer her some type of commitment?

She shook her head. No, if he couldn't offer her a commitment because he wanted to, then she was not going to force it out of him. The last thing she wanted was for him to feel trapped in a relationship he had never really wanted.

Ten

After Angie loaded her car and was ready to go, she checked the classified ads in the morning newspaper for both help wanted and apartments for rent. Next she grabbed the Seattle phone book and looked for employment placement services and made some phone calls to set up appointments. It was almost noon by the time she had finished and was ready to leave.

She did one last walk through Mac's house to make sure she had everything. She was no longer sure exactly what she felt. She seemed to be more numb than anything else. This was the right move to independence that she should have taken when she left Portland. Yet there was an emptiness inside her, a void she didn't think could ever be filled again—a void where Tyler Farrell had resided. But there was still a place deep inside her where she knew he would always be. With a heavy heart she reached for the phone.

"I'm all packed and ready to leave, Mac."

"Are you sure you're doing the right thing?"

"Yes, I'm sure."

"There isn't anything I can say to change your mind?"

"No. This is what's best for me. I'll call you this afternoon as soon as I get checked into a motel. I've made some appointments for tomorrow with placement services and I have a couple of apartments I want to look at this afternoon."

She concluded her conversation with her brother, then looked around one more time to make sure she hadn't forgotten anything. A wave of uncertainty swept through her as she stepped outside. She had gone over the ground in her mind so many times, but she could not keep the thought from surfacing again. Should she give Ty one more chance to make a commitment?

She had toyed with the notion of just asking him for one, but had rejected it for the same reasons that had plagued her earlier. She kept coming back to the same conclusion. She wanted him to freely make a commitment of his own accord because it was what he wanted, not because she had pushed him into it. If it couldn't be something he willingly volunteered, then it wasn't to be.

She closed the door. The clicking sound had a finality to it as if it symbolically represented the closing of the door on that chapter of her life. The old adage said that when one door closed in your life that another door would open somewhere. All you had to do was find that other door. She walked toward her car. A single tear trickled down her cheek. Hopefully she would find the right door to her future, one that would provide her the permanent happiness that had so far eluded her.

A wave of despair swept through her. It would be a future without Tyler Farrell.

Ty pulled into the parking lot, turned off the engine and sat there without making any attempt to get out of the car and go into his office. His meeting that morning had been nothing more than a blur of voices moving in and out of his mind without any one comment pausing long enough for him to digest it. He had declined lunch so that he could retreat to his office and try to sort things out.

He had spent a restless night, but he wasn't sure why. Dark clouds of confusion had assaulted his senses as he tried to sleep. Bad feelings...conflicted feelings...emotions he had never experienced before...all of them swirled around inside him leaving him totally unsettled. Something was very wrong and he didn't know what. The only thing he could be sure of was that it all had to do with Angie and him—and the future.

He knew she had been trying to tell him something, to make him understand something, but what? Had he just not understood what she was saying or had he chosen not to embrace the thought? Waves of trepidation had plagued him through the night and continued in the daylight hours. A little tremor made its way through his body. He shook his head in an attempt to ward off the troubling thoughts. He wanted to believe it was only his imagination, that there wasn't any problem, but he knew that wasn't the answer.

He climbed out of his car and slowly walked into the building. As he crossed the lobby Ellen handed him his phone messages. He looked up from reading his messages as he entered his office. His gaze immediately fell on the angry countenance of McConnor Coleman who was perched on the edge of the desk staring at him. His throat went dry. His stomach tightened into a knot as the anxiety welled inside him. Whatever was going on, it was not good.

"Mac? Is there something you need?" Ty placed his attaché case on the credenza behind his desk as he tried to maintain a casual manner in spite of the foreboding shoving at him.

"Yes—" Mac slid off the edge of the desk and stood facing Ty. "You can tell me what you did to Angie that made her decide to leave."

A hard jolt of shock charged through Ty followed immediately by an intense jab of fear. "Leave? Angie is leaving?" Everything inside him turned to a quivering mass of jelly. He couldn't keep the emotion out of his voice as he tried unsuccessfully to wrap his mind around what Mac was saying. All he could manage was to repeat what he had already said, the words uttered in an unmistakably shaky voice. "Angie is leaving?"

"Don't play cute with me."

Ty could not shake away the bewilderment that swirled around inside him. Panic and a true sense of urgency filled his every word. "What are you talking about?"

"How could you have led her on like that? Playing fast and loose with her emotions, treating her like she was just another of your party girls."

"Angie's leaving?" Somehow he had to get his mind locked into what had happened. "Where is she going?" Panic welled inside him, expanding and growing with each successive minute.

"I don't know exactly. But because of you she's

taking the next ferry to Seattle and will be checking in at—''

''No!'' The reality of Mac's words suddenly sank in, the meaning popping into crystal clarity. ''I won't allow it!''

Ty charged out of the office, leaving a startled Mac staring after his retreating form. A combination of dread and alarm pushed him blindly toward the parking lot and his car. She had decided to go back to Portland with Caufield. There couldn't be any other explanation for her leaving. She was headed toward Seattle to check in with him at his hotel.

Had he truly lost her? His determination slammed into high gear. One thing was for sure—he wasn't going to simply give up and let her go. He loved her. Without her his life was nothing and the future had no meaning. He had to find her and once he found her he would somehow have to find the right words to make her stay.

Ty instinctively knew he was somehow responsible for her making that decision. *Somehow responsible...* that was a laugh. He didn't need to think very hard to have the reality push through the wall he had built to protect his own vulnerability. It had to do with commitment—facing up to his feelings, to his fears, a true and lasting relationship and what the future held. It had to do with love, with giving her his unconditional and undying love.

He drove directly to Mac's house hoping to catch her before she left. As soon as he turned the corner onto Mac's street he saw that her car was gone. A second wave of panic washed through him. He was too late. His heart pounded. So many times it had pounded when he was around her, but this time it was fear rather than passion. He drove straight to the ferry dock. He had to get on the same ferry. If she got to Seattle before him, he might never find her again—at least not in time.

The bitter taste of adrenaline filled his mouth as he approached the car staging area. It was filled and the cars were already driving on board. He saw her car as she drove on. There was no way he would be able to make it on the ferry in his car. He frantically looked around, then made a sudden turn into the restaurant parking lot across the street—the one with the sign clearly stating that the parking lot was for restaurant patrons only and all others would have their vehicles towed away. A towing and impound charge would be a small price to pay if he could reach her in time.

If—there was no *if*. He had to succeed. He could not allow any other outcome. There were no exceptions.

He ran into the ferry building and down the hall toward the foot passenger boarding area.

"Hey…don't close that door." He raced toward the entryway and squeezed through just in time. He allowed a moment to breathe a sigh of relief. Now all he had to do was locate Angie on a large ferry boat filled with hundreds of passengers, maybe even more than a thousand, and he only had thirty-five minutes before the boat arrived at the dock in downtown Seattle. It was a formidable task, but one he had to accomplish. There weren't any options. There was no such thing as *almost*.

She was his life and he had allowed her to go away. *Allowed*…that was absurd. A more accurate description would be that he had driven her away by stupidly indulging his fears and hiding from reality rather than telling her how much he loved her. Absolute and total panic churned in the pit of his stomach. A sick feeling tried to work its way up his throat. He tried to formulate an efficient plan for locating her, but his mind was so muddled he couldn't think.

He shook his head and set his jaw in determination. He had to get his fears under control. He needed to bring some calm logic to the problem so that he could resolve it.

The vehicle deck. He would try that first in case she had decided to stay in her car. And even if she hadn't, if he could locate her car he would know where to find her as the ferry docked. It was a bright red color, a shiny metallic red, and the car had Oregon license plates. He had seen which lane she was in when she drove aboard. At least he knew which side of the boat to search. He raced toward the vehicle deck and squeezed through row after row of parked cars. He finally spotted her car. He tried the doors. They were unlocked.

Logic…he had to get his emotional upheaval under control and apply logic. Where would she have gone? He looked around and located the door closest to her car that led upstairs to the passenger decks. He took the stairs two at a time. His pulse raced and his heart pounded. He was desperate to find her before the ferry docked. Once she returned to her car he would only have a few brief minutes before she would be clear to drive away. He needed more time than that.

He checked the line at the cafeteria and the surrounding tables where people were eating, but she wasn't there. He stayed on the main deck, hoping his guess about her location was right. The panic welled inside him again and the fear coursed through his veins. He methodically made his way from the back of the ferry toward the front, carefully scanning the groups of passengers for any sight of her. He had never been so frightened in his life or so panicked. He had to find her. She was his life, the one single thing that mattered above and beyond everything else.

Angie leaned against the railing at the front of the ferry, the breeze ruffling through her hair as she stared at the Seattle skyline in the distance. Several tears stained her cheeks. She quickly wiped them away with her fingers. Somewhere out there was a future for her— a place to live, a career. And maybe that special someone? She closed her eyes. A sob caught in her throat. No one would ever be able to replace Tyler Farrell in her heart.

She opened her eyes and stared at the horizon. Ty was the past. She had to look to the future. She could not continue without a commitment and Ty had been unwilling to offer one. She preferred to end the relationship now rather than hear empty words that would make a breakup even more painful at a later date.

She glanced at her watch. They would be docking in about twenty minutes. She would check into a motel, then find a job. It was a straightforward and simple plan of action. A place to live, a job and a new start on her life. She thought when she broke her engagement with Caufield that it was a clean start to a new life, but she had been wrong. She never dreamed she would become involved in a new relationship. Now she would start again, only this time she would stick to her goals. She wouldn't allow—

"Angie?"

Her breath froze in her lungs and she stopped breathing for a few seconds. The voice came from behind her, a voice she knew so well. A shiver ran up her spine and rippled across her skin. Was the voice real or had she wanted to hear it so much that she imagined it? She hoped against hope she would see Ty standing behind her.

She slowly turned around. Her heart skipped a beat. He looked so sexy, so strong, so sure of things. But his eyes held a level of panic she never would have associated with him. He had followed her on the ferry. But how did he know? Had he seen her leaving? Did he know about her plan?

She didn't have time for any more thoughts. He pulled her into his embrace and held her tightly against him. He folded her in his warmth. She felt so safe and secure in his arms. She loved him so much, but she had to know they had a future together. She couldn't accept a one-sided relationship. She couldn't commit to that relationship if she was the only one making a commitment.

She swallowed the lump in her throat as she tried to speak. ''What...what are you doing here?''

''That should be my question. Mac said you were leaving.'' Total relief soared inside him. He had found her before they docked in Seattle. Then the dark cloud overshadowed his elation. Was it in time? And now that he had found her he needed to...

He tried to get his thoughts straight, but could only blurt out the first thing that came to his mind. ''You don't need to go back to your ex-fiancé. I make a good living. You can stay here. I can take care of you.''

He continued to hold her in his arms. He didn't want to ever let go of her for fear she might disappear. Somehow he had to convince her to stay. He placed a loving kiss on her forehead as he gently caressed her shoulders. His words were a soft whisper, words he had already said but couldn't stop himself from saying again. ''I can take care of you. I want to take care of you.''

Her moment of contentment disappeared. Had she heard him correctly? Take care of her? She had allowed herself to jump to the conclusion that he cared about her in the same way she cared about him and it had turned out not to be true. She would not make that mistake again. She would not misinterpret his words, make them mean what she wanted them to be—make assumptions.

She pulled back from him and looked up into his face. ''You can take care of me?'' She stepped out of his embrace. As long as he held her in his arms she knew she wouldn't be able to think straight.

''Having someone take care of me is not what matters. It isn't what I want out of life. I can take care of myself.''

He reached out for her again, but she sidestepped his efforts. He furrowed his brow as the confusion swept across his face. ''Then why are you going back to him? Back to Caufield?''

A moment of stunned silence hung in the air before she could muster a response. Her surprise clung to her words. ''What makes you think I'm going back to Caufield?''

''Well…you told me he went to Seattle and checked into a hotel and that he had come here to take you back to Portland with him. When Mac said you were packing up and leaving, that you intended to catch the ferry to Seattle, I naturally assumed…well, what else was I to think?''

Angie glanced toward the horizon, at the Seattle skyline and the ferry dock growing closer and closer. She took a steadying breath and plunged into what had been left unsaid when she and Ty were last together. There was no reason to hold back, no reason to hold out hope that he would willingly offer what she wanted most to hear.

"Caufield offered me a commitment, a promise for the future. But what he wouldn't do was allow me to be who I am, to pursue my career, to find fulfillment within myself and my capabilities. He wanted me up on some sort of ivory pedestal where my activities could be controlled by him which would include going to the country club, donating my time to his mother's favorite charity and being a decoration on his arm when the occasion called for it. It was a suffocating prospect."

She paused for a moment as she shook her head and pursed her lips. "It's not exactly what I'd call the basis for a lifetime partnership of equality or a happy marriage. I couldn't live with that type of a relationship, with the restrictions..." she made eye contact with him "...any more than I could live with a relationship that didn't include a commitment."

Ty swallowed hard. He wasn't sure exactly what to say or how to respond to her words. "Then where are you going?"

"I'm going to find a job and my own place to live. I have a couple of appointments tomorrow and I've circled several apartments for rent in the newspaper that I need to look at."

Again confusion clouded his thinking. "But what does that have to do with right now? Where are you going to stay tonight?"

The announcement came over the loudspeaker sys-

tem telling all drivers to return to their cars immediately.

Angie looked toward the dock, then at Ty. A sense
of urgency surrounded her words. ''I need to return to
my car. You need to get to your car, too. We'll be
docked in a couple of minutes.'' She turned toward the
door going from the outside deck to the inside area of
the ferry.

''Angie, wait. Where are you going? Where can I
find you? Where will you be tonight?''

She ran from the deck, past the cafeteria area, then
headed for the stairs leading down to the vehicle level.
She disappeared in the crowd of people attempting to
return to their cars, but Ty knew where she had parked.
He had to get to her car before she was able to drive
off the ferry. If he missed her on the vehicle
level…well, he didn't want to think about it. It was not
acceptable. He could not allow it.

He shoved his way through the crowd toward the
stairs. As soon as he reached the vehicle level he
skirted his way around the parked cars, most of them
with occupants and the motor running waiting for the
car ahead of them to move forward. He reached her
car, yanked open the door and slid into the passenger
seat. The shock spread across her face at his sudden
appearance.

He gulped in a couple of deep breaths to calm his
breathing. ''I don't care where you're going, but wher-
ever it is I'm going with you. We have to talk.''

''What about your car? You can't abandon it here
where it will be blocking the other cars trying to
leave.''

''I had to leave my car in the restaurant parking lot
across the street from the ferry dock on Bainbridge.

There wasn't time for me to get on with my car so I boarded as a foot passenger.''

The car in front of them started moving forward. She put the car in gear and followed. Her mind raced to put together what was happening. Ty had followed her on the ferry, but for what specific purpose? To ask her not to leave? But without a commitment, it wouldn't matter. She knew she had to stand firm on that point. It was very important to her.

He interrupted her thoughts. "As soon as you get out of here, pull over on the first side street you come to. We have to talk right now. It can't wait."

"Talk about what?"

"About us..." He took a steadying breath in an attempt to calm his inner fears and shove aside his anxieties. "About the future."

"That's what I'm doing here, Ty. I'm taking care of my future. I've explained it to Mac. He understands." Her insides quivered and trepidation welled inside her. She felt trapped. At that moment, as much as she wanted a commitment from Ty, she needed to get away by herself and clear her head of the stifling confusion.

"Well, I don't understand. Maybe I'm just too dense. You're going to have to explain it to me. I want to know where you're going and exactly why. If you explained it to Mac, then you can explain it to me, too."

Her hackles stood on end. He sounded as if he was dictating to her, telling her what to do. How had everything gotten so out of control and gone so wrong? Every step she took put her in a bigger mess than she had been before. The last thing she wanted was a painful confrontation, but she didn't seem to be able to escape it. Perhaps confronting him now would be better than later. Now would allow her to make a clean break of it. She knew she couldn't handle a long drawn-out confrontation. She loved him too much.

Leaving without talking to Ty, however, had been the coward's way out. She had been suffering misgivings about the way she had handled the decision. She turned into a parking lot a couple of blocks down the street from the ferry dock.

Angie turned in her seat until she faced Ty. "Okay. What do you think we have to talk about?"

Ty tried to swallow his fears so that he could appear calm and in control. But as much as he wanted it to be so, he knew he had failed miserably. His fear of losing her, of her no longer being part of his life and his future, totally overshadowed his deeply held fear of making a commitment.

He grasped her hand. He craved the physical contact, the warmth and security of her touch. He needed the courage it gave him, the courage to say what he should have said long before then. To say what was in his heart.

"Angie..." His throat went dry. He was about to say the most important words he had ever spoken, words that would have an impact on his entire future and the rest of his life. He had to say them and say them quickly before he lost his nerve again. He pressed the back of her hand to his lips.

"Angie...I love you." Once those most important and feared words were out of his mouth it was as if the dam had burst. Words tumbled out in an almost frenzied manner as if he couldn't say them fast enough. "I love you very much. I'll work very hard to make sure you're never bored. You'll never feel neglected or be taken for granted or patronized. I would never hold you back from being all that you can be, from accomplishing whatever you want.''

Angie's insides quivered so violently that she was sure her entire body must be visibly shaking. No words had ever sounded as marvelous as what Ty had just said. The jubilation rose inside her, shoving everything else aside. Tears of joy filled her eyes and threatened to overflow.

''Are you sure, Ty? You're not just saying that because it's what I want to hear?''

''I'm saying it because I mean it. I want us to spend the rest of our lives together. When Mac told me you were leaving I was so scared. I have never been as panicked before in my life. I knew I had to do everything in my power to stop you. I can't imagine what the future would be like without you.''

He leaned forward and kissed her. ''I love you, Angie.'' His voice dropped to a whisper, the words coming directly from his heart. ''Come home with me. Be part of my life and let me be part of yours for all the years ahead.''

Total elation bubbled inside her. ''Oh, Ty...I love you so much. I've been so scared, so afraid that you didn't love me. And when you wouldn't make a commitment to us, to our relationship and our future, I felt I had to leave so I could make a clean break and get on with my life—a life I knew would always be empty without you.''

''I'm so sorry, Angie. I didn't mean to hurt you like that. I tried to convince myself that a verbal commitment wasn't necessary, that we both knew we would always be together, but that was wrong. A relationship needs a firm foundation in order to last and that requires clearly stating what that foundation is.''

He squeezed her hand. "I want this relationship to have the strongest foundation possible and that includes marriage."

He brushed another kiss against her lips. "Marry me, Angie. Do me the honor of being my wife."

"Yes...oh, yes! I'll marry you." She flung her arms around his neck. "I love you." She had never been happier in her life and the future had never looked brighter.

"There's only one thing left to do."

She looked at him quizzically. "What's that?"

"We have to tell Mac right away so he can get this entire thing settled in his mind and stop jumping down my throat in that over-protective big brother way of his."

"You're right. Let's turn around and take the ferry back."

He flashed a teasing grin. "And maybe get my car out of the restaurant parking lot before they have it towed away." The grin slowly disappeared to be replaced by a look of total adoration. "I love you so much."

She placed her hand against his cheek. "Forever."

"Yes, forever."

Epilogue

Angie replaced the phone receiver in the cradle, then turned toward Ty and Mac. "Well, Mom cried, then said we had to start immediately on wedding plans even though we haven't set a date yet. She's envisioning a large ceremony with the invited guest list equaling the population of Portland."

Mac scrunched up his face. "Ouch! That sounds expensive."

"Yes, and much too elaborate for my tastes. Ty and I have discussed it and we both want a small, simple wedding—"

Ty quickly added his thoughts. "And a month-long honeymoon." He turned his attention to Mac. "That's going to leave you solely in charge of everything until we get back." He flashed a teasing grin. "You know, all those *people things* that you always try to avoid."

"I'll manage to muddle through." Mac paused as if

a thought had just occurred to him "—but you can't be gone any longer than a month."

"I hate to interrupt the wedding and honeymoon discussion," Angie said, her gaze darting between Mac and Ty, "but I'd like to change the topic."

She adopted a very businesslike persona. "We have company expansion plans to deal with, decisions that need to be made so that we can go forward smoothly with as little disruption to the work flow as possible."

A soft chuckle escaped Mac's throat. "I knew you were going to be a tough taskmaster. You haven't been a partner in this for even a week yet and already you're calling the shots." His expression turned all business. "All right, boss. What do you suggest we do first?"

Angie shot a teasing grin toward her brother. "My first executive decision is to declare it lunchtime. I'm hungry and you're buying!"

Mac beamed at his sister. "It will be my pleasure."

Ty pulled her into his arms. "That was an excellent decision, Mrs. Farrell."

"I'm not Mrs. Farrell yet."

"I know, but I like the way it sounds." Ty brushed a soft kiss against her lips.

Angie's whispered words were for Ty's ears only. "So do I."

*   *   *   *   *

Get swept up in

Emilie Rose's

captivating new tale...

BREATHLESS PASSION

On sale February 2005

Lily West was struggling to get her business off the ground when she was offered a tantalizing proposal— pose as millionaire Rick Faulkner's fiancée and all her dreams could come true. But she was a tomboy from the wrong side of the tracks—*not* a socialite dripping charm. So Rick became Lily's tutor in the ways of sophistication...and a red-hot attraction ignited between these star-crossed lovers!

Available at your favorite retail outlet.

Coming in February 2005
from

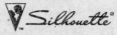

Margaret Allison's
A SINGLE DEMAND
(Silhouette Desire #1637)

Cassie Edwards had gone to a tropical resort
to find corporate raider Steve Axon, but ended up
losing her virginity to a sexy bartender instead.
Cassie then returned home to a surprise:
her bartender *was* Steve Axon! Mixing business
with pleasure was not part of her plan, and
Cassie was determined to forget that night—
but Steve had another demand....

Available at your favorite retail outlet.

If you enjoyed what you just read,
then we've got an offer you can't resist!

Take 2 bestselling
love stories FREE!
Plus get a FREE surprise gift!

COMING NEXT MONTH

#1633 A RARE SENSATION—Kathie DeNosky
Dynasties: The Ashtons
Veterinarian Abigail Ashton wasn't looking to lose her virginity while staying at Louret Vineyards—then again, she hadn't counted on meeting sexy cowboy Russ Gannon. After a night of unexpected passion, Russ assumed he wasn't Abby's kind of guy. Little did he know, he'd caused a rare sensation that Abby didn't want to end.

#1634 HER MAN UPSTAIRS—Dixie Browning
Divas Who Dish
Marty Owens needed to remodel her home and asked handsome contractor Cole Stevens for help, never guessing their heated debates would turn into heated passion with one thing leading to another…and another…. Yet Marty knew that the higher she flew the harder she'd fall, and wondered if her heart could handle falling for the man upstairs.

#1635 BREATHLESS PASSION—Emilie Rose
The only son of North Carolina's wealthiest family, stunningly sexy Rick Faulkner needed Lily West's help. Before long, their platonic relationship turned into white-hot passion, and now Lily, a girl from the wrong side of the tracks, wanted her Cinderella story to last forever….

#1636 OUT OF UNIFORM—Amy J. Fetzer
Marine captain Rick Wyatt and his wife, Kate, were great together—skin to skin. But beyond the bedroom door, Rick closed Kate out emotionally, and she wanted in. When an injury forced Rick out of uniform, Kate passionately set out to win the battle for her marriage.

#1637 A SINGLE DEMAND—Margaret Allison
Cassie Edwards had gone to a tropical resort to meet with corporate raider Steve Axon but ended up losing her virginity to a sexy bartender instead. Then Cassie returned home to a surprise: her bartender *was* Steve Axon! Mixing business with pleasure was not part of her plan and Cassie was determined to forget that night—but Steve had another demand….

#1638 BOUGHT BY A MILLIONAIRE—Heidi Betts
Chicago's Most Eligible Bachelor, millionaire Burke Bishop, wanted a child and hired Shannon Moriarity to have his baby. Knowing that Burke would make a wonderful father, Shannon had agreed to keep things strictly business—but soon she realized Burke would make the perfect husband. But would Mr. Anti-Marriage agree to Shannon's change of terms?

SDCNM0105